Flying Into Darkness

By Diane E. Izzard

ISBN: 978-0-9970065-3-7

Dedication

To my husband Bill whose passion for flying inspired this story.

Acknowledgements

Many thanks to my family and friends for their encouragements and being my biggest fans.

Much appreciation to Debby Eye for performing the final edit. I am always grateful for her amazing talent and attention to detail.

Special thanks to Mary Jo Manus for her keen eye and amazing skills. Your input is always appreciated.

One

Jose lay on the soft, sandy soil looking up at the star-filled sky as an airplane took flight and roared overhead. He could see the lights from the brightly lit runway. He imagined the wonderful destinations the airplanes were flying to. A place full of happy children living in big homes, with green, lush yards, and plenty of toys. The sound of his mother's voice interrupted his dream.

"Jose, it is time for bed! Come inside and get cleaned up."

"Yes, Mama!" he yelled back. Jose's mother spends her days and part of her evenings working two jobs to make ends meet. She doesn't get to spend a lot of time with Jose, since she cleans homes for some of the more wealthy residents and works as a maid at a beach front hotel. At eleven years old, Jose does his part to help with the finances. He works in the sugarcane fields with his uncle during the summer months.

Jose crawled into his small bed and listened to the sounds in the darkness: the faint roar of a jet engine in the distance and the occasional hum of a car engine as it drove by. He leaned over his bed and retrieved a flashlight and a book hidden underneath, then flipped through the pages of the tour book he had found in a ditch near the hotel where his mother works. As he turned the page, the flashlight illuminated a beautiful park with monuments. The book was full of places located in America. Large sparkling lakes, mountain peaks covered in snow, and a desert filled with flowering cactus stared back off the pages at him. Even though he was exhausted from working all day in the sugarcane fields, he couldn't sleep. At eleven o'clock at night he desired more out of life than living a dull, non-eventful existence in a small four room wooden house with his mother and Nana. Next door to him lived his Aunt Maria, Uncle Marcus, and his two younger cousins. He planned to escape this life, to go to a place were dreams are

1

made real. If he was to have any fun this summer he needed to act soon. He decided as he drifted off to sleep that tomorrow night he would leave the only place he has ever lived and fly to America where dreams come true, or so he hoped.

The next day was like every other. He woke at daybreak to the screams of his mother; "Get up Jose!"

Jose's uncle honked the horn of his beat up pickup truck as he impatiently waited for him. His mother handed him a breakfast burrito as he raced out the door. Another hot day in the sugarcane fields awaited. Knowing this would be the last time for a while that his hands would ache from cutting the sugarcane eased his mind.

He arrived home as the sun was just starting to set, tired and covered in dirt. He drenched himself with a hose outside his house to clean up before supper. He walked into the kitchen where Nana was busy preparing a wonderful smelling meal.

"Jose, you're getting water all over the floor!" She threw a towel at him to dry himself and the floor.

Nana scooped out a bowl of stew from the stove and placed a chunk of bread on the table in front of Jose. His mouth watered at the sight of the scrumptious food. A day in the fields had left his stomach empty. He hurriedly ate so he could finish his chores. He jumped up from the table and started to run outdoors.

"Jose, put your dirty dishes in the sink if you're finished," Nana yelled before he was out the door.

He did as requested and slipped outside to feed the chickens and collect the eggs from the day. As the sun slipped below the horizon he was greeted by his mother after a long day picking up after tourists. He held up the basket of eggs he carried. "The chickens did good today. They produced eighteen eggs."

"That will make a good addition to your allowance." Jose always sold the extra eggs to the neighbors. She kissed him on the forehead and ruffled his hair. Even though she was tired she sensed something was wrong and asked, "Are you feeling okay?"

"Yeah" he replied. "I'm just tired and plan to go to bed early tonight." He hated deceiving his mother.

Jose waited until his mother was busy doing laundry, then quietly filled a small burlap bag with everything he would need for his adventure. He grabbed a pair of clean shorts and t-shirt, the leftover bread from supper, a few dollars he had managed to save from selling eggs, a flashlight, and lastly his picture book of America. He hid the bag underneath his bed to keep it out of sight from his mother. Then he climbed into bed and pretended to be asleep. He listened for the house to become quiet. When all he could hear was the sound of the jets flying overhead he quietly grabbed his burlap bag from underneath the bed. He stepped on a chair and climbed out his open bedroom window and heard dogs barking in the distance, probably excited over some critter they'd found. He walked the short distance to the airport perimeter and made his way to where there was a small hole under the fence, squeezing through the opening. He walked toward the airport terminal building, staying in the shadows so he wouldn't be seen. He waited, hidden from view, for what seemed like an eternity. In actuality it was only thirty minutes before a plane landed and parked near him on the tarmac. He watched as the plane was offloaded. The cargo door opened and all the cargo was removed. It wasn't long before a baggage carrier full of bags pulled up beside the plane to be loaded for the next group of people leaving Belize. He kneeled down on the ground beside a parked truck and waited for his opportunity. The guy loading the luggage started arguing with someone by the baggage carrier. Jose realized that this was his chance to sneak on the plane without being seen. He leaped up from his hiding place, ran the short distance across the tarmac, and jumped on the conveyor belt being used to load the bags. He rolled off the conveyor onto the steel belly of the airplane and quickly disappeared inside the cargo area. He squeezed behind some wooden pallets loaded with cargo. He quietly waited and listened to see if anyone saw him board the plane. He could still hear the loud voices from the guys arguing. The yells grew closer and he feared he would be discovered. Then he heard a loud thump! The yelling stopped. What was that? He glanced around the pallet full of cargo. He couldn't believe his eyes. He heard the cargo door slamming shut. He was thrown into darkness.

He pushed what he had just witnessed out of his mind. He excitedly whispered to himself, "I did it!" There was a sudden jar as the plane was pushed away from the terminal. His eyes slowly adjusted to the darkness surrounding him and then he heard a moan. He wasn't alone. He felt his way out of his hiding place, bumped into something on the floor, and looked down. Even in the darkness he knew it was the body he had heard fall to the floor. He listened intently for any sign of movement. The moaning stopped. The engines roared to life and he braced himself as the airplane barreled down the runway. He held onto the crate in front of him as the airplane floated up from the runway, then lifted steeply up. The pressure in his ears increased as the airplane gained altitude. Then, before he knew it the plane was leveling off and the engines throttled back.

Jose moved away from the body in front of him and found a place to curl up on the belly of the airplane. The hum of the engines kept him company. The temperature started to plummet. His light shorts and t-shirt weren't enough to keep the cold out. He started to shiver uncontrollably, and needed to find something to wrap himself in to stay warm. He removed his flashlight from his burlap bag and turned it on, then gasped at the sight of the man laying in a pool of blood on the floor. He cautiously stepped over the body and found where the suitcases were stacked. He unzipped the first bag he could reach and rummaged through the few clothes packed inside it to determine if any would fit him. His hand scraped against something underneath the clothes. He pulled out a plastic bag and shined the light on it. To his delight it was filled with jelly beans. He helped himself to a couple of bags of the delicious candies and stuffed them in his burlap bag for later. He zipped the suitcase back up, then cautiously searched for another suitcase with clothes his size. He stumbled across a large duffle bag, and unzipped the bag, pushing the contents aside. He

4

made enough room for him to fit inside amongst all the clothes and climbed inside, wrapping the garments snuggly around him. He slowly stopped shivering. Thoughts of his mother entered his head. Did she realize he was gone yet? He had left her a note on his pillow so she wouldn't worry. The note indicated that he had gone on an adventure and would be home in a few days. He didn't explain where he was going, since he didn't know himself. Now warm he could no longer stay awake. The constant drone of the engines lulled him into a deep sleep.

Jose was jarred awake as the airplane landed with a hard thud. He started to panic at the realization that he had fallen asleep. The cargo door would be opening at any moment. He grabbed his burlap bag and tucked it inside the duffle bag with him, zipping the bag closed so he would stay concealed. He left just enough of an opening for him to breathe. It became quiet as the engines wound down. Then he heard a loud clunk as the cargo door opened. He braced himself and hoped that he wouldn't be discovered.

The duffle bag he was hiding in was suddenly lifted into the air. He fell with enough force to make him moan in pain. Then another bag was thrown on top of him. He feared he may suffocate from the weight. Then he was on the move. He swayed back and forth as the luggage was transported to the terminal. He came to a sudden stop. The bag crushing him was finally lifted. He drew in a deep breath of air through the small opening, then felt himself being hurled through the air, landing with a thud onto the baggage carousel. He waited a few seconds then unzipped the bag. He cautiously peered through the opening. Everyone around him appeared busy. He hurriedly opened the bag the rest of the way and jumped to the floor, dragging his burlap bag behind him. He quickly hid behind some boxes, then spied a door off to his left. He securely tied his burlap bag around his waist, and without hesitation, quickly stepped through the door.

Jose came to a sudden stop. There were people crowded around the baggage carousel waiting for their bags. Jose searched for a way out of the building before he was caught. He forced his way around all the weary travelers. Then he saw how he could escape without being seen. There was a large group of people gathered off to the side. A man held a sign that read Tropical Tours. Jose quickly blended in with the group. He tried to look like he belonged, standing close to several children that appeared to be about his age. The group started to move and he moved with them. No one seemed to notice him. The group was herded onto a large bus. He found a seat near the back.

A boy about his age sat next to him and placed his backpack on the floor. "Hi, my name is Levi," the boy cheerfully announced.

"I'm Jose," he said, and placed his burlap bag on the floor in front of him.

"Is this your first time going to Disney World?" Levi asked.

He couldn't believe his ears. The bus was headed to Disney World! He tried to hide his excitement. "Yes," he answered, smiling from ear to ear. His dream was truly coming true, he thought to himself.

This was Levi's second time, so he proceeded to share with Jose which rides were the best. Jose glanced out the window as they drove past many large buildings. The bus picked up speed as they got on the highway. There were so many cars. The city landscape slowly turned to a more rural setting, with palm trees and vast fields. He read several large colorful billboards advertising surf shops and restaurants.

Jose was starting to think they would never arrive when the bus exited the highway. A few turns later the bus stopped in front of a huge hotel. He eagerly glanced out the window and was amazed at the sight of a large waterfall with lush tropical green plants surrounding the entrance of the hotel.

There was a lot of commotion as everyone on the bus gathered their belongings, stood up, and started toward the exit. Jose followed Levi off the bus and into the hotel lobby. It was more magnificent than any hotel his mother had ever worked at. There was a large aquarium in the lobby with all kinds of tropical fish swimming around.

"See ya around," Jose told Levi. He knew it was just a matter of time before someone figured out he didn't belong with the group.

He took in his surroundings. The center of the hotel was open with a beautiful fountain spewing water. Coins glistened off the bottom of the fountain. Jose watched as a little girl threw a coin in the water. "Make a wish," Jose heard the little girls parents say. Jose thought that was strange behavior. How would throwing money in the water make a wish come true? He continued to explore the hotel. He looked up as glass elevators raced toward the sky, taking guests to their rooms. He walked toward the back of the hotel lobby and found an area where breakfast was being served. He suddenly realized how hungry he was. He watched as people picked up a plate and placed food on it. No one seemed to ask for any money. He stepped in line and followed the person in front of him. He couldn't believe all the food! He loaded his plate with eggs, bacon, fruit, a muffin, and some yogurt. He found a small table by the window overlooking the pool. He devoured most of his meal, but decided to save the muffin for later. He drank a large glass of orange juice which tasted so sweet. He rarely had orange juice at home because it was too expensive. On his way out of the dining area he grabbed an apple and an orange. He hid them in his burlap bag along with the muffin.

Jose discreetly wandered around the lobby and waited for the elevator to become free. The elevator door opened and several people exited. He rushed inside and pressed the fifth floor button before anyone could join him. The door closed and he started to rise quickly. He looked down through the glass and watched as the people in the lobby grew smaller. The elevator door opened and he peered down an empty hall. He walked past a few doors then noticed a maid's cart. It was like the one his mama used. It had been left outside a room with the door ajar. He cautiously approached and peered inside the room. The maid was busy

7

cleaning the bathroom. He quietly sneaked inside and hid under the bed. The vacuum started and he laid perfectly still in his hiding place as the maid cleaned the carpet around him. Then he heard the door slam shut.

He waited for a little while longer to make sure the maid wasn't going to return or someone else enter the room. Once he determined it was safe, he crawled out from under the bed. He opened the door to the closet. It was empty. It appeared the room was currently vacant. He looked out the large plate glass window and couldn't believe his eyes. There was a large lagoon below him. He beamed with delight at the sight of the enormous water slide. He wandered around the room taking inventory. The refrigerator was stocked with water and soda. On the counter was several packets of coffee and tea, along with a bag of popcorn. Next, he looked in the bathroom and found a small bottle of lotion, shampoo, mouthwash, and some smelly bars of soap. This was much nicer than the hotel his mother cleaned. He stood on his tiptoes at the sink and reached for the faucet, then turned the water on and let it run through his hands. He splashed some water on his face and used a crisp, clean, white towel, still warm from the dryer to remove the water from his hands and face. He made himself at home and plopped on the bed. The mattress was so soft his small body was swallowed up by the enormous bed. There was a large flat screen television along the wall in front of him. He jumped off the bed and found the remote at the base of the television, then pressed the red power button. The screen came alive. He pushed more buttons and the channels changed. He crawled back into bed and found a channel with cartoons, and watched as the characters danced around the screen. With a full stomach, he fell fast asleep to the soothing sounds of laughter coming from the television.

He awoke to voices outside his hotel room. It took him a little while to remember where he was and he started to panic, fearing he may be discovered. He rolled off the bed and slid underneath to hide. The noise moved down the hall and he breathed a sigh of relief. He crawled back on top of the bed, deciding his next move. His stomach ached with hunger and he remembered the muffin he had hidden in his bag from breakfast. He grabbed a soda from the refrigerator and eagerly drank while he ate the muffin. On the night stand was a booklet with everything to do at Disney World. The guide showed how to get to the monorail that would take him to Disney World. He was reluctant to leave the safety of the room, but was dying to go on the rides. He found a small note pad by the bed and grabbed it, along with his burlap bag. Cracking open the door to the room, he looked in both directions down the hall to make sure it was clear. He carefully placed the pad between the door and the jamb so when the door closed it wouldn't lock. He had learned this trick helping his mother clean rooms. Excited at his prospects, he walked with confidence to the elevators. His adventure had just begun.

Two

Carter awoke to the sound of his cell phone ringing. "Hello," he mumbled sleepily. He had been up most of the night investigating what appeared to be another gang related murder on the South side of Miami.

"I'll be right there," he responded as he became more awake. Carter had been with the Miami police force for twelve years. At the disappointment of his father, he became a cop following four years of college where he studied business. It didn't take long for him to make detective. This morning was like many mornings in Miami with a new murder to investigate. But this time it was a little different. The dead body was inside an airplane at the Miami airport.

Carter hurriedly brushed his teeth, splashed water on his face, and dressed in cotton blend trousers and button down cotton shirt. It was too hot for a tie in the Miami summer heat. He liked to dress professionally, and looked sharp in his tailored clothes which showed off his lean, muscular body. He didn't drive the standard police issue four door sedan. Instead, he preferred a black 435hp Mustang confiscated in a drug operation. Today the Mustang weaved in and out of rush hour traffic as he made his way to the Miami International Airport. He arrived at the crime scene, joining Chip, the medical examiner, and Rosa Lopez, his partner.

"Don't you look sharp today!" Rosa teased.

Carter smiled, "You only wish you could look this good," he replied. Getting down to business he asked, "What can you tell me Rosa?"

"Well, we believe the victim's name is Julio Sanchez." With gloved hands she showed him the Belize Airport employee badge that hung from the victim's neck.

"Chip, any idea how he was killed and whether it happened in Belize or on American soil?"

"It appears he died from a stab wound to the neck." Chip moved the victim's neck sideways to show Carter the stab wound. "Since it hit a major artery it didn't take long for him to bleed out."

Carter looked at the pool of blood around the victims body. "Any idea how long he has been dead?"

"It's hard to tell. The extreme cold temperatures of the cargo area at altitude would affect the body temperature. I would have to guess around five hours."

"Rosa, did you check the plane's itinerary?"

"Yes, it left Belize at 11:35 PM and arrived in Miami at 7:05 AM."

"That would mean our victim was probably killed in Belize inside the cargo area of this airplane. I will contact the Belize authorities and make them aware of the situation."

"There is one more thing you may be interested in," Rosa spoke up. "There appears to be a footprint in the victims blood." She pointed to the floor of the cargo area covered in blood.

"The print is too small to be an adult," Carter responded with a puzzled look on his face.

"Do you think there was a kid inside the cargo area when the victim was killed?"

"Is it possible someone may have witnessed the murder or that there was a stowaway?" Carter thought out loud, not expecting a response. "I'm not going to share the footprint evidence with the Belize authorities just yet. Why don't you pull the airport security camera footage and see what you find?"

Rosa left to talk to airport security while Carter searched the cargo area for any more evidence. He weaved his way around the pallets of cargo still waiting to be offloaded, shining his flashlight toward the floor. "What do we have here?" He leaned down to take a closer look and found two more bloody footprints similar in size to the one found by the body. He was now convinced that someone had been hiding behind the pallets of cargo when the murder took place, but wondered where they were now.

The Miami summer heat was quickly making the temperature inside the cargo area unbearable. "Chip, the body is all yours. I have seen everything I need to see for now."

The body was neatly secured in a body bag and hauled to the waiting medical examiner vehicle.

Carter left the crime scene and started walking back across the tarmac to where his Mustang was parked. On his way he spotted Rosa approaching with a handful of CDs.

"I never knew there were so many cameras in the airport," Rosa said, showing the enormous stack of discs to review for any signs of their stowaway witness.

"Looks like you have your afternoon cut out for you!" Carter laughed.

Rosa sarcastically replied, "Thanks for offering to help. Did you discover anything else?"

"As I matter of fact I did. I found two more bloody footprints behind the pallets of cargo. That could only mean one thing. There was definitely another person in the cargo bay area on the airplane with the victim," Carter said.

"My thoughts exactly. I'll meet you back at the station," Rosa said.

Carter arrived at the station and pushed aside the piles of unsolved murder cases on his desk to clear a space to work. He took out his notes from the crime scene and searched for a phone number for the Belize police chief.

Carter received very little additional information from the Belize authorities. If the Belize police chief knew anything about Julio Sanchez he was keeping the information to himself. The chief indicated there was no missing person report filed for a Julio Sanchez. He would check Julio's address and whether he was employed at the airport. Now all Carter could do was wait.

Carter hung up the phone and looked over at Rosa pouring through the security footage. "Have you found anything yet?"

"Well, the video shows the luggage being removed from the airplane as usual, that is until the baggage handler discovered the dead body. Then, with a look of panic, he rushes out of view of the camera. I assume to notify someone. He returns a few minutes later and all hell breaks loose. The plane was immediately swarmed by security personnel. The luggage had already been offloaded onto the baggage carrier and driven away by the time the body was discovered."

"Do you have the security footage of where the luggage was taken?"

Rosa sorted through the stack of CDs on her desk. "Here, this one is labeled 'baggage area'." She handed Carter the disc.

Carter slid the CD into his computer. He intently watched the screen as each suitcases was removed from the baggage carrier and thrown onto the conveyor belt. Then something caught his eye. He reversed the video and slowly watched one bag in particular as it moved down the conveyor belt. "There!" He froze the video.

"Did you find something?" Rosa asked.

"Yeah, look at this."

Rosa looked at his computer screen and couldn't believe her eyes. The image showed a little boy climbing out of a duffle bag. "What's the time stamp on the video?"

"07:45 AM. That aligns with the time the plane was offloaded."

Excited at the possibility of finding a lead, Carter jumped up and hurriedly grabbed the stack of security disc from Rosa's desk. He sorted through them until he found one labeled 'baggage terminal'. He popped it into his computer, looking for the carousel where the Belize bags were being claimed by their owners.

Rosa leaned over his shoulder and yelled, "There!" She pointed at a boy on the screen that was dressed in the same shorts and t-shirt as the one seen climbing out of the duffel bag.

Carter slowly moved the footage forward, trying to keep an eye on the boy. He disappeared into the crowd of people. "Where do you think he went next?" Carter asked, thinking out loud and not expecting an answer.

Rosa rolled her eyes and said, "He could've gone just about anywhere from the airport but I bet he joined this tour group that he disappeared into. See the guy holding the sign?" Rosa pointed to the computer screen, "Tropical Tours."

Carter quickly searched for the phone number for Tropical Tours. Rosa eagerly listened as Carter talked to the Tropical Tours dispatch office. Carter hung up the phone with a smile across his face. "Are you ready for a road trip?"

"What did they say?" Rosa asked impatiently.

"The bus took a group of people to a Disney World resort hotel. Now if I was a kid from Belize, that would be the first place I would want to go. I will call the hotel and see if they can email us their security footage from this morning. If we can confirm the kid got off the bus at the hotel we should be able to find him before he disappears again."

While they waited for the hotel video they ordered pizza for lunch. They pigged out on a pepperoni pizza and finished viewing the remainder of the security footage from the Miami airport, hoping to find more clues. Carter viewed the video of the boy exiting the baggage area several more times and printed the best picture of the kid he could find. The boy was skinny, very tan from the Belize sun, with shaggy, black, curly hair. He had some sort of a bag wrapped around his waist. Carter felt sorry for the young boy, knowing how scared he must be in a strange country.

What would make a kid so desperate as to risk his life sneaking into the cargo bay and flying here? Carter thought to himself. He watched again as the boy quickly hid from view and disappeared into the terminal area. The security footage continued to run and something caught Carter's eye. The guy off loading the bags onto the baggage carousel placed one of the bags on the floor out of the way from the other bags. Carter continued watching the screen. After a few minutes another man appeared on the screen and picked up the bag left on the floor. He walked out of view of the security camera and disappeared with the bag in his hand.

"That is interesting," Carter said out loud.

"What is it?" Rosa asked.

Carter rewound the video. "Watch this guy off load the bag from the luggage carrier, place it on the floor, then walk away. Then a few minutes later another man picks up the bag and takes it with him."

"You're right, that is interesting. Do you think they are smuggling something in from Belize?"

"I don't know, but it might be worth having the Drug Enforcement Unit take a look to make sure nothing illegal is going on." Carter picked up the phone to share his suspicion with Chappy, an officer working undercover in the drug gangs.

Rosa listened to Carter's end of the conversation, which didn't amount to much.

Carter finally hung up the phone. "Chappy said there is a new drug showing up on the streets but he hasn't been able to determine how it is being distributed. He's going to take a look at the video footage and have the two guys at the airport monitored for anymore suspicious deliveries."

"Do you think there may be a connection between whatever was in that bag and our dead guy?" Rosa asked.

"You might be on to something. Let's say our dead guy is an honest airport worker in Belize who happens to stumble into a drug smuggling operation. He confronts whoever is placing the bag full of drugs in the airplane cargo area. The guy suddenly panics, is fearful of being caught, and kills our dead guy so his secret can remain safe."

"Not a bad theory but we have no way to prove it. It could've been someone's dirty laundry in that bag after returning from vacation." Rosa said.

"I have this feeling something will turn up," Carter said. A "ping," alerted him to a new email. It was from the Disney Resort hotel he had contacted about their security video. He double clicked to open the file and played the video footage from the hotel lobby. He fast forwarded until the time stamp reflected the time the bus arrived. Rosa and Carter stared intently at the screen, watching as a bus pulled up in front of the hotel. They watched as each person exited the bus.

They had just about given up hope that the boy was on the bus when Rosa yelled, "Stop, there he is!" He was one of the last people to get off the bus and then he quickly disappeared from view.

"Now what? We know he got off the bus but he could be anywhere."

"Now it is time to show the captain what we have and get permission to go on a road trip to find our witness. If we drive up to Orlando tonight we could possibly find the kid before he leaves the hotel," Carter explained.

Three

Jose followed the signs leading to the monorail entrance. He hid behind a column and watched as a line of eager passengers formed waiting for the monorail to arrive. He patiently waited until a family with six kids arrived, then jumped in line behind them, trying to blend in. He started talking to the boy in front of him. "Hi, is this your first time to the park?"

"Yes, we are from Iowa. Where are you from?"

Jose hesitated and then said, "Miami."

"We just arrived a few hours ago. I can't wait to ride the roller coasters with my dad."

Jose smiled, but deep down he was sad he had no family to share this experience with. He never knew his father. His mother had told him his father had died before he was born. Looking at the happy complete family saddened him and reminded him of what he didn't have.

The monorail rushed into the station with a blast of wind. The excitement bubbled over as eager children waited to board. The monorail doors opened and the line started to move. The family in front of Jose showed the attendant their Disney passes and started to walk through the turnstile. Jose stayed close with the boy he had been talking with as he edged forward. He managed to slip through without being asked for his ticket.

Jose found a window seat and anxiously waited for the doors to close and the monorail to speed away from the station. With a sudden jolt he was on his way. He watched as the beautiful flowers and waterways flashed by his window. The monorail came to a stop at the entrance to Magic Kingdom. He stood with the other tourists and exited the monorail. The anticipation of what lay ahead was almost too much for him to bear. He made his way down the ramp, restraining himself from running all the way. He followed the crowd to the Magic Kingdom.

Jose couldn't believe he had actually made it inside the park. He was overwhelmed by everything around him. Cinderella's Castle towered in front of him. Goofy and Mickey Mouse came joyfully walking down the street toward him. He spent the next few hours standing in lines with the other thousands of tourists to enjoy the thrill of a lifetime. He rode Space Mountain through the dark enclosure with lights flashing as he whizzed by. He went on the Jungle Cruise. He got splashed from the elephants squirting water from their trunks and spooked by the rhinoceros that popped up beside the boat. The water felt good and cooled him off from the hot humid day. He raced a car on the Tomorrowland Speedway and laughed until he couldn't stand it anymore on the Mad Tea Party. After watching the night parade with the floats draped in magical colored lights, he made his way back to the monorail entrance with the masses to ride back to the hotel. He was so tired he struggled to stay awake on the journey back. He followed the other weary passengers back to the hotel.

He rode the elevator to the fifth floor and cautiously entered the hallway to his room. The hall was quiet. He managed to make it to his room without being noticed. The note pad he had placed on the lock was still in place, which meant no one entered his room while he was gone. He pushed open the door. Once inside, he placed his burlap bag on the bed and took off his worn tennis shoes. He collapsed on the bed, but hunger pains kept him awake. He hadn't eaten since   waking up from his nap. He retrieved the apple he had placed in his bag from breakfast. He took a big bite and juice ran down his chin. He grabbed a soda from the refrigerator. Then he remembered the bag of popcorn in the kitchen. He placed the unopened bag in the microwave and pushed the popcorn symbol on the display panel on the microwave. The microwave came to life and the popcorn started to pop. A loud beep signaled the popcorn was done. The butter flavored aroma surrounded him and he drooled with anticipation.

He opened the bag to let the steam out. When it was cool enough he stuffed a big handful of popcorn in his mouth. He washed down the popcorn with soda. By the time he finished the entire bag he thought his stomach may explode. He washed the butter from his face and hands before climbing into bed. He pressed the power button on the television remote and sounds of children laughing filled the room. The noise kept him company and he fell fast asleep.

***

Carter and Rosa finally received approval from the captain to travel to Orlando to find their witness. The ride was tiresome after an already long day.

To keep Carter awake, Rosa chatted on. "Have you ever been to Belize?" she asked.

"As a matter of fact I have," Carter answered.

"I didn't know you were such a world traveler. What did you think of the place?"

"Well, from what little I can remember, it was absolutely beautiful. I went for spring break with some of my frat brothers during my senior year in college. We stayed pretty drunk the entire time we were there."

"Must be nice being from a wealthy family."

"It's not as great as you may think. Yes, Dad bought me the trip as an early graduation gift. But the gift was tied to certain expectations once I graduated. Dad always assumed that once I graduated I would join him at his financial investment firm. That's not what I wanted, though. The idea of sitting in a stuffy office all day long talking to clients wasn't my idea of a dream job. Instead, I decided to apply to the police academy. You would've thought I had told my Dad I was moving to Alaska, he was so upset."

"Since you're his only son, I'm sure he just wanted what he thought was best for you."

"I know, but working in finance just seemed so boring. That was the last way I wanted to spend the rest of my life. I know it made my family a lot of money but there's more in life than working in a job you hate just to make money."

"Wow, this is a side of you I didn't know existed. I figured you joined the police force so women would fall at your feet." Rosa laughed.

"Very funny. In actuality I think I would attract more women if I was rich." Carter loved hearing Rosa laugh. She had a contagious laugh that just made you want to laugh along with her.

They finally pulled up to the hotel where Jose was last seen in Orlando just before 1 AM.

"I don't know about you, but I'm exhausted," Rosa said.

"As soon as we talk to the front desk clerk to determine if the boy has been spotted, we can crash for the night."

Carter flashed his badge to the young man behind the counter. "We're looking for this boy. Have you seen him?"

"I just reported to work at midnight and have seen very few people since I arrived," he responded.

Carter realized he wasn't going to get anywhere tonight. Frustrated, he asked, "Do you have two rooms available?"

The desk clerk typed on the computer and said, "Yes, there is a room with two queens and next door a room with a king size bed."

"That sounds perfect."

"How would you like to pay for them?"

Carter flipped his charge card on the counter. They were handed the room keys for the second floor rooms. On the ride up the elevator Carter said, "I'll meet you in the lobby at eight. Hopefully by then someone will have reported to work that can help us find our witness."

"You're killing my beauty sleep," Rosa smiled.

"You'll survive," Carter joked. Rosa was a beautiful brunette, with curly hair she often tamed by pulling back in a ponytail. She was from Puerto Rico and had glorious bronze colored skin and big brown eyes. Carter often thought that if they didn't work together, he would ask Rosa out on a date.

Jose woke with a start. It was light in his room and he rarely got to sleep until the sun came up. Then he remembered he wasn't at home. He felt a little homesick. He actually missed being awaken up by his mama yelling at him and handing him a breakfast burrito on his way out the door. His stomach grumbled at the thought of food. He remembered the breakfast he had yesterday. He climbed out of bed and went to the bathroom. He hurriedly splashed water on his face, brushed his teeth with his finger, and put on the clean clothes he had brought with him. He wrapped the burlap bag with all his precious possessions back around his waist. He opened the door, cautiously peering down the hall to make sure it was clear. He carefully placed the pad back in the door jamb so it wouldn't lock. Then he rode the elevator to the ground floor. Once again there was a line of people filling their plates. He helped himself to a big stack of pancakes which he drowned in syrup. He looked for an empty table and found a small one hidden behind a large plant, that no one was using. As he ate he looked around at all the happy faces. Families with children chatted about their plans for the day. He wondered whether he had made the right decision to leave his family.

As he eavesdropped on the conversations around him, he heard a man and woman talking. What they were saying caught his attention. He listened closely.

"We can start with interviewing the staff to see if anyone saw the boy yesterday."

"Don't forget to review the video from the elevators to see if it captured the kid."

Were they talking about him? Jose wondered. He hunched down behind the plant so he wouldn't be seen and waited for the two people talking to leave, then slowly crept from behind the plant. He grabbed a danish, a muffin, and an apple and placed them in his burlap bag. He decided it wasn't safe to stay in this hotel any longer. He found a side exit and pushed the door open, stepped into the hotel parking lot and started walking, but to where he wasn't sure.

Jose was smart enough to stay off the main roads and walked through the many hotel and business parking lots. After walking for several hours he found himself in a residential neighborhood. That's when he noticed a black SUV with tinted windows driving slowly down the street. Jose hid behind some palm trees as it drove past. He turned and headed in the opposite direction from the vehicle. As the sun started to sink on the horizon Jose found himself in a large park. There were people jogging, walking their dogs, and children enjoying the playground, without a care in the world. Exhausted from the heat and long walk, Jose found a shaded park bench and took a seat. His stomach ached from lack of food and he was very thirsty. He rummaged through his burlap bag and found the muffin from breakfast he had stashed. He ravenously ate it, and then the apple, as he watched a father pushing his son on the swing set. Jose missed having a dad to do things with. His uncle always watched over him but it wasn't the same as having a dad. He was too busy with his own children to have time to spend with him.

Jose's thoughts were interrupted by the sound of a soft voice.

"Is anyone sitting here?"

Jose looked up at the beautiful smiling face of a young lady. He shyly responded, "No."

"My name is Angelia. What is yours?"

"Jose."

"I have an extra peanut butter and jelly sandwich if you would like one?" Angelia held out the sandwich and a bottle of water for Jose to take.

Jose eagerly drank the water to quench his thirst. Then he slowly munched on the sandwich.

Angelia visited this park every evening, passing out food to the homeless and looking for runaways. She was actually Sister Angelia. She helped operate a children's shelter just down the road. "Are you visiting from out of town?" she asked.

"Belize," slipped out of Jose's mouth before he realized what he was saying.

Angelia couldn't believe her ears. Surely Jose must have family nearby, but his skinny unkempt appearance indicated otherwise. "Belize, you're a very long way from home. I've only seen pictures of your homeland but it looks to be a beautiful place."

Jose pictured the crystal clear ocean waters and lush tropical plants around his home. He suddenly was very homesick.

Sensing Jose's sadness Angelia asked, "Are your parents here with you?"

Jose looked at his feet and responded, "No."

"Are you staying with relatives?" Angelia pursued.

Jose hesitated, wondering whether he should lie. Angelia seemed very nice and Jose decided he could trust her. "No, I flew here by myself."

Angelia feared she may have found another runaway. "What a brave boy you must be. Do your parents know you arrived safely?" Angelia continued to pry.

"It's just me and my Mom. She doesn't know I flew here," Jose said looking at his feet. He continued to slowly eat the peanut butter and jelly sandwich. He found it easy to trust this woman he had just met.

"She must be very worried about you. I don't live far from here. I take in children who need a place to stay. You can spend the night with me if you like. You can use my phone to call your mother to let her know you are safe. How does that sound?"

Jose swallowed the last bite of his sandwich before answering. "I guess I could stay with you just one night."

"Good. I have more food at home if you're still hungry."

Jose looked up and the same black SUV with the tinted windows drove by again. He hid behind Angelia until it disappeared down the street.

"We better get home before it gets dark. My house is just a few blocks away. Will you walk with me?" Angelia urged Jose, holding out her hand for him to grab.

Jose stood without a word, watching to see if the black SUV returned. They walked down the sidewalk, crossed the busy street, and walked just a few blocks. The homes in the neighborhood were built close together. They were only a few feet apart. There were practically no yards. Jose was relieved when Angelia turned up the walkway of a small two story house. They entered through a screened in porch. There was a wooden swing hanging from the ceiling, on the right side of the porch. Jose thought it would be fun to swing on it.

Once inside Angelia said, "Jose, I'd like for you to meet Joey, Cody, and Mark."

"Hi," Jose shyly replied.

"You'll be bunking with them tonight. Mark, can Jose have the bottom bunk?"

"I guess," Mark replied, leery of his new roommate.

"Jose, is there a phone number where I can reach your mother to let her know you're staying with me tonight?"

"Yes, my uncle has a phone." He proceeded to tell her the phone number.

Jose followed Angelia into the kitchen where she dialed the number. She handed Jose the phone after it started to ring. He was scared his mom was going to be furious with him for what he had done. He waited patiently for someone to answer the phone. The ringing suddenly stopped and Jose heard a woman's voice.

"Is this Aunt Maria?" Jose asked quietly.

"Yes. Jose is that you? Are you okay? Your mother has been worried sick. Where are you?"

Jose relayed, "I'm in Orlando and I'm fine. I'm staying with Angelia tonight."

"Put Angelia on the phone so I can get your address. I'll send your uncle to pick you up," Aunt Maria replied.

Jose's uncle was a very strict man and Jose was not thrilled to hear he would be coming to get him. "My aunt wants to talk to you."

Jose handed the phone to Angelia. She reassured Maria that Jose was in good hands and gave her the address where he was staying. She also indicated she would have to contact the police before handing Jose over to anyone. Jose couldn't hear his aunt's response to Angelia, but based on her face it must not have been nice. Angelia hung up the phone and looked over at Jose with a smile on her face. "Did you get enough to eat?"

"Yes ma'am."

"Well, why don't I show you to the bathroom so you can get cleaned up before bed?"

"I heard you tell my aunt you were going to turn me over to the police," Jose said, fearful of what they would do with him after sneaking on the airplane.

"That's just for your own protection. Since I don't know your family, the police will make sure it's safe to turn you over to your uncle. Do you understand?"

"I guess."

"Let's get you cleaned up. I'll find a night shirt and some clothes for you to wear."

Jose followed Angelia to the back of the house where there were boxes of clothes stacked against the wall. In the mounds of chaos, Angelia magically went directly to a box, pulling out a few items. "How about these jeans and this shirt?" She held up the jeans against Jose's leg to determine if they would be long enough. Satisfied with her selection she handed the clothes to Jose.

Jose smiled when handed the shirt. An emblem of an airplane diving from the sky was on the front of the shirt.

"Oh, here we go," she said as she reached into another box. "You can wear this large t-shirt to sleep in tonight."

Jose took the t-shirt, holding it up to himself. It hung down to his knees.

Angelia next showed Jose where the soap and towels were located. She turned on the shower for him. "When you are done cleaning up, your bedroom is just next door."

Jose stepped into the bathroom and slowly slipped off his soiled clothes. He cautiously stepped under the water to make sure it wasn't too hot. He scrubbed himself all over with the soap and rinsed off. He turned off the shower and dried himself with the towel Angelia left for him to use. He could hear Angelia talking to someone. He stood quietly and listened.

"Let him get a good night's rest and you can pick him up in the morning."

It sounded like Angelia was talking to the police. "They're going to take me away in the morning," Jose whispered to himself.

Jose dressed in the jeans and t-shirt he was given. He then gathered up his dirty belongings in the bathroom and walked to the bedroom where he found Joey, Cody, and Mark waiting for him.

"That's where you'll sleep tonight," Joey spoke up pointing to the lower bunk.

Jose placed his belongings on the bed. Then he sat on the edge. "How long have you been staying here?" Jose pried.

"I've been here almost a year," Joey said.

Cody spoke next. "Alex and I are brothers and have been here a few months."

"Where are your parents?" Joey asked.

Jose looked at the floor and quietly responded, "My mother is in Belize. I don't have a father."

"My mom is in prison," Joey added. "What do you have in that bag?" Joey pointed to Jose's burlap bag resting on the bed.

Jose pulled the bag tight against his chest as if it was his lifeline.

Joey sensed Jose's uneasiness and said, "I didn't mean anything by it. Whatever you have in there is yours. I was only curious."

Jose relaxed a little and remembered he still had the jelly beans he had taken from the suitcase in the cargo area of the airplane. He rummaged through his bag and pulled out a couple of bags of jelly beans. "I have these if you would like some," Jose offered.

The boys eyes lit up and they each grabbed a bag of jelly beans.

Before they had a chance to enjoy any Angelia stuck her head in the door. "It's time for bed boys. Put away your things and say your prayers." Angelia waited for each boy to get in bed.

Jose took off his jeans and laid them on top of his bed. He climbed underneath the covers and placed his burlap bag beside him in the bed.

Angelia turned out the light and Jose waited for the other boys to fall asleep. He knew he would be arrested if he stayed till morning.

Four

Carter and Rosa finished a quick breakfast, then headed to the front desk to find someone who may have seen the boy. Carter introduced himself to the woman now manning the desk. "Is there someone we can talk to about this boy? He may be hiding in your hotel." Carter held up the photograph for the woman to see. "Have you seen this boy?"

"He doesn't look familiar to me. Let me contact the manager. He might be able to help you." She lifted the phone off the receiver, pressed three buttons, and talked to the person on the other end of the line. "Two police detectives are here and would like to talk to you about a missing boy." She hung up and said, "He'll be right out."

Before Carter could say another word a man approached from down the hall.

"Hi, my name is Mike Rogers. I think I spoke to you on the phone about video footage from our security camera." Mike extended his hand. "Why don't we go to my office? We can talk there."

They were offered a seat, but Carter felt more comfortable standing. "Mr. Rogers, we appreciate you sending us the video. It was very helpful. It showed this boy getting off a tour bus at your hotel yesterday morning." Carter showed him the picture of the boy. "We have reason to believe he maybe hiding in the hotel. Do you have any cameras located in the elevators that might show where the boy went after he left the lobby?"

Mike clicked a few buttons on his computer keyboard. "Here are the videos from yesterday from the two elevators. Let's take a look and see if the boy shows up in any of the footage." Each time the elevator door opened he slowed the video to focus in on the faces as they entered the elevator. It didn't take long before the face of the boy appeared.

"There he is!" Carter yelled.

They continued to watch the video. The boy exited on the fifth floor.

"Rosa, why don't you continue to view the video to determine if he shows up again. I'm going to the fifth floor to see if anything looks suspicious," Carter explained. "If I need access to a room I'll give you a call."

Carter rode the elevator to the fifth floor, looking up at the camera in the corner of the car. He wasn't thrilled with heights, and looked away as the lobby grew smaller as the glass car raced upward. The elevator door opened and Carter looked in both directions down the hall to decide which way to go first. A family with two noisy, unruly children approached. They talked loudly, excited about going to the pool. Carter smiled courteously as they passed. "Lord help me if I ever have children," Carter muttered under his breath.

Carter slowly made his way down the hall, looking for anything out of the ordinary. He had just about given up when something caught his eye. He looked closer and noticed an object stuck between the door and the jamb. Carter pulled on the door and it opened. He removed his gun from the holster, not knowing what to expect. "Police! Is anyone here?" he yelled.

There was no response. He searched the room. The bed had been slept in. There were two soda cans and the remains of a popcorn bag in the garbage can. The closet was empty. He used his cell phone and called Mike Rogers' office.

"Can you tell me if anyone stayed in room 525 last night?"

After a few seconds of clicking noise Mike Rogers responded, "The room has been vacant for the last two days. Why did you find something?"

"Yes, I think this is the room the kid stayed in last night. Did you find anymore video of him on the elevator?"

Carter heard Rosa speak up and then her voice came over the phone. "Carter, I just found video of the kid exiting the elevator in the lobby this morning at 8:00. We must've just missed him on our way to breakfast."

"Well, with any luck he'll return to the room where he has been staying on the fifth floor. Why don't you take a look around the lobby and pool area? I'll stay up here in case he comes back." Carter closed the door to the room. He placed the note pad back in the door jamb so the door wouldn't lock, and waited impatiently for the kid to return.

***

As a courtesy, Carter called the Orlando police department. He forwarded a copy of the boy's photograph to the Orlando police chief and asked to be contacted if he was found. The afternoon slowly went by with no sign of the boy. Rosa stayed in the lobby hoping to catch him returning. By eight o'clock at night they were both starved and frustrated.

Rosa called Carter on his cell phone. "I think the boy has given us the slip. He either saw us and got spooked or just left."

"That was my thought, also. I know you must be as starved as I am. Why don't we grab a bite to eat in the hotel restaurant and figure out where to go from here?"

Carter kept an eye on the lobby while they ate, hoping the boy would appear. It was now almost ten o'clock.

"We can either drive back tonight and admit defeat or stay one more night and hope something turns up in the morning," Carter said.

"I vote for staying one more night. This is the closest thing I've had to a vacation in years," Rosa laughed.

Carter's cell phone suddenly rang and he quickly grabbed it so as not to disturb the other patrons in the restaurant.

Rosa listened intently as Carter quietly talked on the phone.

"Great! I'll be right there." Carter smiled at Rosa as he disconnected from the call.

"What is it?" Rosa impatiently asked.

"It may just be our lucky day. That was the Orlando police chief. He just received a call from a shelter that takes in children. A boy matching the description of our photograph is staying just a few miles from here."

Carter quickly paid for their meals and they rushed to his car.

✳✳✳

Jose quietly slid into the jeans Angelia gave him. He gathered up his burlap bag and tied it around his waist. He really liked Angelia and was sorry to have to leave. Just as he was about to slip out the bedroom door, the doorbell rang. He held his breath, hoping the other boys didn't wake up. Then he heard Angelia open the door and say, "Officers, it's very late. Can this not wait until morning?"

Fear gripped Jose. The police had come early to arrest him. He must leave now. He peeked out the bedroom door and quietly stepped into the hall. He sneaked out the back door while Angelia was busy talking to the officers at the front door. A privacy fence blocked his exit out of the back yard. He found a gate leading to the street side. He opened it and hid in the shadows of the trees and bushes. The officers were still standing on the front porch talking to Angelia. He made his way to the street and took off running as fast as he could, away from the police.

Jose looked back and was relieved to see he wasn't being followed. He stopped to catch his breath at the street corner. Before he realized it, someone grabbed him from behind. They put their hand over his mouth so he couldn't scream. He was lifted off the ground and thrown into the back of the black SUV with the dark tinted windows.

***

Carter tried to reason with Sister Angelia. "Let me see the boy so I can at least confirm he's the boy we are looking for."

"This can't wait until a decent hour in the morning? The boy is sleeping. I told the police I would bring him to the station in the morning."

"I know you must think I'm insensitive, but this boy may have witnessed a murder. His life could be in danger."

"The only danger he's in tonight is from you." Exasperated with his persistence, Angelia finally relented. "Come in and take a seat in the living room. I'll wake Jose up so you can talk to him."

Carter and Rosa sat on the sofa and waited for Angelia to return.

Angelia quickly reappeared, "He's gone! He couldn't have gotten far. I just put him to bed a little over an hour ago."

Carter and Rosa leaped up from the sofa and ran outside. They looked down the street just in time to hear car tires squealing in the distance. "Get in!" Carter yelled.

He did a u-turn in his Mustang, racing toward the direction of the noise. When he reached the intersection, he came to an abrupt stop. He could see tail lights in the distance quickly disappearing from view. He floored the accelerator, trying to catch up with the car.

"Hurry, you're losing them!" Rosa yelled. "They turned right up ahead."

Carter took the turn, barely slowing down. The tail lights were nowhere in sight. "Where did they go?"

Carter slowly drove down the street looking for any signs of the car. He couldn't believe he had lost them. He pounded the steering wheel in frustration.

"I noticed at that last intersection there was a streetlight camera. Let's go to the police station. Maybe we can get a closer look at the car we were following. With any luck we might get a license plate number," Rosa said.

Carter knew the Orlando police department wasn't going to be happy that they were interfering in their jurisdiction. This was going to be another long night.

Before Carter could turn around and head in the direction of the police station, his cell phone rang. It was Chappy, the drug enforcement officer who was performing surveillance on the baggage handlers at the airport. "Did you find out what was in the luggage that was being handed off?" Carter asked.

"As a matter of fact I did. I had a couple of guys stake out the baggage area this morning. They watched for the suitcases off the next airplane arriving from Belize. The same guys were working in the baggage as before. They set a bag aside just like they did yesterday and my guys followed it. It was taken to lost and found and then another guy picked it up. We waited until he walked outside the airport with the bag in hand and grabbed him."

"So what was in the bag?" Carter impatiently asked.

"Jelly beans."

"Did you say jelly beans?"

"Yes. At first I wondered if we just arrested a candy smuggler. I had our lab test the jelly beans for any controlled substances. They found a synthetic derivative to heroine. After questioning the mule all afternoon he didn't give up much. But this is the scary thing. He said there were some bags missing from the shipment yesterday and his boss wasn't happy. Do you think your kid could have picked up some, not realizing it wasn't candy?"

Rosa watched as Carter's face turned white.

"I've got to run. Thanks for letting me know," Carter said.

"Letting you know what?" Rosa asked.

Carter suddenly made another u-turn.

"Where are we going?"

"Back to the shelter to make sure the kids didn't get any jelly beans from Jose." Carter explained to Rosa what Chappy had told him.

The lights were still on at the house. The door flew open as soon as they arrived.

"Did you find him?" Angelia anxiously asked.

"No. I need you to make sure none of the boys staying at your house were given any jelly beans from Jose."

"Okay," Angelia hesitated. "Can it wait until morning? They are still asleep."

"No, it can't wait."

"You'd better wait here. If the boys see it's the police asking they may not cooperate. Their relationship with the police hasn't been the best."

"Understood," Carter said. He watched as Angelia quietly entered the back bedroom and turned on the light.

A short time later she returned with three bags of jelly beans. "The boys said Jose gave them these. They said they hadn't eaten any."

Carter and Rosa both breathed a sigh of relief. Rosa held out an evidence bag and instructed Angelia to place the jelly beans in the bag. Rosa didn't want to add her fingerprints to the mix already on the bags.

"What's this about?" Angelia asked.

"We think either on purpose, or by accident, Jose took these jelly beans from a bag he found in the cargo area of the airplane he flew on. We believe they are laced with a type of heroine."

"There is no way Jose could have known that the jelly beans were anything more than just that, candy. I can tell after working with these troubled boys for several years which ones are evil and which ones have a good heart. Jose has a good heart and has just lost his way. Find him and return him safely to his mother."

That reminded Carter that they needed to get to the police department to view the traffic camera footage to find the car they were chasing. "Thanks for your help tonight." Carter handed Angelia his card with his cell phone number.

"If you hear from Jose, will you give me a call immediately?" Carter asked.

"Of course, detective. And if you find Jose, please contact me to let me know he's safe?"

"Yes, as soon as we find him I'll let you know," Carter said as he turned to leave.

Five

Jose struggled to get away from his attacker. He bit the hand that was tightly held across his mouth. Then he heard his name being yelled out.

"Jose, stop fighting! It's me, your uncle."

Jose stopped struggling and looked up at the man over him. It was definitely Uncle Marcus and he was very mad. Jose was scared to say a word.

"Why did you bite me?" A speck of blood ran down his finger.

Jose quietly responded, "I didn't know it was you."

"I've been looking all over town for you. Jose, I'd like you to meet Teo. He is my brother and your uncle." He motioned toward the driver. "He has a friend on the police force that told us where you were staying. We were just coming to pick you up when I saw you running down the street," Uncle Marcus explained.

Uncle Teo pulled off onto a side street and parked. He reached into the back seat and forcefully grabbed the burlap bag from around Jose's waist. "Let's see what you have in here, kid." He took everything out of the bag and threw it on the floor of the SUV. He pulled out the one bag of jelly beans Jose had saved for himself.

"Where are the rest of the jelly beans?" Uncle Teo demanded.

Jose stuttered and said, "I gave them away."

"Who did you give them to?"

Jose couldn't understand why he wanted the jelly beans so badly. "I'm sure you can buy some more at the store?"

"I don't want the jelly beans from the store," he angrily responded. "I want to know what you did with the jelly beans you stole off the airplane."

Jose was shocked. How did he know he had taken them from the suitcase in the cargo area?

"Speak up!" Uncle Teo yelled.

"I gave them to some boys I met."

"And where can I find these boys?"

"They are at the house I was staying in tonight."

Uncle Teo started the car and quickly turned around. He drove in the direction they had just came.

"Think this through Teo, and don't do anything rash. The police are going to be looking for Jose. Let's just return to Miami," Marcus said, trying to calm his brother down.

"Not without the other three bags," Teo demanded.

The SUV stopped in front of Angelia's home. The lights were on in the kitchen. "I want you to go in there, get the jelly beans, and come right back out. Do you understand?"

Jose nodded up and down. He looked at Uncle Marcus for approval before stepping out of the vehicle.

"Just take your time and don't get caught," Uncle Marcus instructed.

"If you don't come out in five minutes I'm coming in after you and someone is going to get hurt. So do not waste any time," Uncle Teo said.

Jose stepped out of the car, almost stumbling as his foot hit the pavement of the sidewalk. He quietly approached the front door and turned the knob. It opened easily and he crept inside. He saw Angelia seated at the kitchen table. He walked toward the back bedroom, but came to a sudden stop at the sound of Angelia's voice.

"Jose, what are you doing? Are you all right? I thought something may have happened to you." Angelia reached down and hugged Jose so tightly he could hardly breathe.

Jose finally spoke up. "I can't stay. My uncle is waiting for me in the car. I just stopped by to pick up some jelly beans I left. Then I have to leave."

Angelia looked out the window at the vehicle parked by the curb. "Why don't I go out and introduce myself to your uncle and invite him inside for something to drink?"

Jose grabbed Angelia's arm to stop her. "No, you can't do that. He might hurt you."

"Jose, I know about your jelly beans. The police already came and took them."

"I have to give them the jelly beans or they might hurt you."

"I have an idea. I happen to have a jar of jelly beans in the kitchen. I'll fill up three bags and tie a bow around them just like the ones you had. Then I'll give them to your uncle. He won't know the difference."

"Okay, but we have to hurry. He said if I wasn't back in five minutes he was coming in."

Angelia rushed to the kitchen and grabbed three clear plastic bags. She opened a drawer and pulled out some ribbon and a pair of scissors. Then she saw Detective Carter's card laying on the counter. She picked up the phone and dialed his number while she scooped some jelly beans in the bag.

"Detective Carter, this is Angelia. Jose is here with his uncle. Hurry!" She hung up the phone before Carter could ask any more questions she didn't have time to answer.

Angelia quickly tied the last bow around the bag. "Do these look like the jelly beans you had?"

"Yes."

"Good. Hopefully he won't be able to tell the difference." Jose reached for the jelly beans and Angelia stopped him.

"I'm not going to let you go back to your uncle. You stay here and I'll deliver them to him."

"He's not going to like that. He might get angry and harm you!"

Angelia reached for the cross she always wore around her neck. She said a quick prayer. "God, please protect me and Jose."

Angelia slowly opened the front door and took a deep breath. She willed her feet to propel her forward, not sure what was waiting for her behind the dark tinted windows of the SUV. Jose watched from the front window as Angelia approached the vehicle. Marcus rolled down the window on the passenger side as Angelia stepped forward. She handed him the three bags of jelly beans.

Jose could hear Teo yelling from the driver's seat. Then there was a loud BANG! Angelia fell to the ground.

Jose took off running as fast as he could toward Angelia. By the time Jose reached her the black SUV was out of sight. Jose could hear sirens as he kneeled down to Angelia on the ground.

"Angelia, are you all right? Don't die!" Jose begged.

Angelia sucked in a deep breath and reached for the cross around her neck. She slowly sat up. "I'll be just fine Jose," she said as she tried to quiet Jose's fears. She reached for Jose's hand and held it to her chest.

"See, there's no blood."

"But I saw him shoot you!"

Angelia held up the cross she wore around her neck. It had a large dent where it stopped the bullet from penetrating her skin.

A smile crossed Jose's face as he held the cross in his hand.

The blue lights were now all around them. Angelia looked up and Detective Carter raced toward her with a concerned look on his face.

"A black SUV with two men inside looking for the jelly beans just shot me before racing away!" Angelia blurted out.

"Are you hurt?" Carter asked frantically.

Angelia once again held up her cross to show the dent. "The good Lord is not finished with me yet," she announced with a smile. "My chest is a bit sore, though."

"Call an ambulance," Carter told Rosa who was standing next to him.

"Can you stand?" Carter offered his hand to help her off the ground.

Angelia grasped Carter's hand firmly. He lifted her off the ground. She winced in pain and grabbed her chest.

"You probably have a few broken ribs. Take it easy and let me help you inside." Breathless, Angelia told Carter, "I would like for you to meet Jose."

Carter had been so focused on Angelia he had totally forgotten about the boy by Angelia's side. A smile crossed Carter's face.

"Jose, it's so nice to finally meet you. You have no idea how happy I am that you are safe."

Jose and Carter helped Angelia to the porch swing. Joey, Cody and Mark, woken from all the commotion, had appeared by Angelia's side.

"What happened?" Joey asked sleepily.

Angelia spoke calmly to the boys. "I don't have time to explain everything right now, but I'm fine. They're going to take me to the doctor just for precautionary measures. But I'll be home again real soon. I'll explain everything then. Father Michael will stay here with you until I return. Do you understand?"

The boys said, "Yes," in unison.

"Good," Angelia said. She took her attention off the boys and looked at Carter. "Can you retrieve the phone from the kitchen so I can call Father Michael?"

"Of course." Carter stepped away and reappeared with the phone in hand.

Angelia quickly dialed the number from memory and waited for Father Michael to pick up. "I am so sorry to wake you. Can you come over to the shelter and take care of the boys for me? I'll explain everything when you arrive."

The whole neighborhood was a buzz of activity. Lights started flickering on in many of the homes as their occupants awoke from all the commotion. The police held everyone back as the ambulance pulled up to the curb. Father Michael arrived and Angelia quickly explained the situation.

Jose held tightly to Angelia's hand the entire time.

Angelia looked into Jose's eyes as the gurney was rolled up her walkway. "Jose, I need you to go with Detective Carter. He'll take good care of you. Don't worry, he's not going to arrest you. He's going to make sure you get back safely with your mother. Do you understand?"

Jose tried to remain brave. With tears in his eyes he nodded up and down. He let go of Angelia's hand as she was loaded onto the gurney and wheeled away.

Carter kneeled down to Jose's level. "I know you must be tired. How about we go to a hotel? I'll actual pay for the room this time."

Jose's face turned red as he realized that Carter knew about the hotel room he had enjoyed for free.

"Jose, I'd like you to meet Rosa, my partner."

Rosa squatted, looking Jose in the eyes with a smile and asked, "How about we get some breakfast before we turn in for a few hours of sleep? I could sure use some blueberry pancakes. How about you?"

An exhausted smile appeared on Jose's face. "I love pancakes. Mama always makes them on Sundays."

"That settles it. We eat some breakfast and then crash from the sugar high for a few hours." There was a tint of pink on the horizon as the sky started to lighten.

✳✳✳

Carter paid for one room with two queen size beds and a sofa. He didn't want to take any chance of Jose escaping. With a stomach full of pancakes it didn't take long for Jose to fall into a deep sleep.

"I'll take the first watch while you sleep," Carter whispered to Rosa. "I'll wake you up in three hours so you can keep an eye on Jose while I sleep for a few hours."

"You know we could just handcuff him to the bed so we can both get some rest," Rosa joked. She looked at Jose lying motionless on the queen size bed. He seemed so small and frail, sleeping soundly in the large bed by himself.

"The poor kid has been through so much the last couple of days he probably won't stir for at least ten hours. Unfortunately, we can't sleep that long. We need to get him back to Miami. Maybe he can tell us who killed the guy in the cargo area and what his uncle's connection is to the drugged jelly beans," Carter said.

"It'll be nice to finally get some answers after chasing this kid all over the state," Rosa said as she made herself comfortable in the bed beside Jose's.

Carter struggled to stay awake. He went over the events of the last two days. He was no closer to solving the case of who killed the person in the cargo area of the airplane. All he had was many more questions. Who was responsible for making and transporting the drugged jelly beans? What was the storage and distribution location of the drugs? How is Jose's uncle connected with all this and where is he currently located? Finally, is Jose just an innocent victim or is he somehow involved? Carter yawned and closed his tired eyes for just a second. That was all it took for him to fall asleep.

✳✳✳

Jose awoke with a start from a nightmare. He was being chased by a man with no face. He sat up in bed and let his eyes adjust until he could see the room more clearly. He couldn't remember where he was at first. He glanced around the room and it slowly came back to him. He remembered Angelia being shot, the police taking him to get something to eat and then to the hotel. The curtains were drawn but the room had a soft glow from the light shining through the crevices. Rosa was asleep in the bed next to him and Carter was asleep in the chair. He suddenly felt trapped and needed to leave. He quietly got out of bed and slipped into his tennis shoes. He opened the door very carefully so as not to make a noise. He stepped into the hall and started walking swiftly down the corridor while he figured where to go next. He turned the corner and bumped into a maid's cart.

"What is your big hurry little man?" Jose heard the maid ask with a strong Hispanic accent.

He quickly thought up a story and blurted it out. "My parents are still asleep and I was just looking for something to eat."

The maid smiled and kneeled down to Jose's level. "I have two boys about your age and they love chocolate." She pulled a candy bar from her pocket and handed it to Jose.

Jose's eyes lit up. He was rarely allowed to have chocolate and eagerly grabbed the candy bar from the maid's grasp.

"How about you sit in here with me while I finish cleaning this room?" She pointed to the chair in the corner of the vacant room.

Jose slowly ate his candy bar, savoring every bite. The maid chatted away with Jose as she cleaned.

"Where are you from?"

"Belize," Jose said as he swallowed a mouthful of chocolate.

"Wow, that is a long way from here. Have you gone to Disney World yet?"

Jose excitedly told her about his day at Disney World and how much fun he'd had.

A loud noise came from down the hall as a door slammed. The thumping of footsteps were heard running down the hall.

Carter came to a screeching stop. He stuck his head in the room where Jose was sitting. "There you are! What are you doing in here?"

The maid spoke up. "I'm sorry. You must be Jose's father. He bumped into me in the hall and was just keeping me company while I cleaned."

Carter wasn't sure what to say, but didn't want to embarrass Jose, so he played the role of father. "Thanks for looking after my son for me. I overslept and was frantic when I saw he wasn't in his bed."

"I have two boys of my own and know how sneaky they can be."

"Jose, we better get going."

"It was nice meeting you Jose. I hope you enjoy your visit in Orlando."

Jose walked beside Carter back to the room. He wondered if he should let his guard down and trust Carter. He didn't act like the police in Belize. He truly seemed to care.

Carter opened the door to their room. "Have a seat while I call Rosa to let her know I found you."

"He's with me," Carter said over the phone. He ended the call and took a deep breath to regain control of his emotions. He looked down at the little, frail boy sitting in front of him.

"You do realize we're trying to help you here? This can be a very dangerous city for a young boy all alone."

Jose gave Carter a defiant look and said. "I can take care of myself. I've been doing so for years working in the sugarcane fields in Belize."

Carter was just starting to know and understand why Jose had run away. He suddenly realized Jose was more than just a murder witness. He knew under that tough exterior was a kid that just wanted to play and have fun like all the other kids.

Rosa stormed into the room and ran up to Jose. She hugged Jose tightly. "You scared the life out of me! I thought someone had kidnapped you again."

Buried in Rosa's, embrace Jose thought of his mama. He felt guilty pretending to be on vacation while she was in Belize working and worrying about him.

Carter broke up the reunion, "We better get on the road if we want to get back to Miami before dark." Carter and Rosa started to pack up their few belongings.

Jose sat on the corner of the bed and watched. He only had the clothes on his back that Angelia had given him. His burlap bag with all his possessions was in the back of his uncle's SUV.

Carter saw the sad look on Jose's face. "I saw a Walmart just down the street. Why don't we stop on our way out, pick you up some new clothes, and grab a bite to eat before we hit the road?"

That brought a smile to Jose's face.

They entered the enormous store and Jose followed Rosa to the boy's clothing section. Carter hung back, keeping an eye on them. Rosa held up a couple of pairs of shorts and t-shirts for his approval. "What do you think of these?"

"I like those," Jose responded.

"Good. Let's get you some clean underwear and pajamas then check out."

Carter paid for the items and took Jose to the mens dressing room. Carter stood outside the door while Jose changed. "What do you want me to do with these?" Jose asked as he held out his dirty clothes to Carter.

"Here, put them in the shopping bag."

Jose did as instructed and then they met back up with Rosa at the McDonald's located inside the store.

Carter asked, "Jose, what would you like to eat?"

Jose looked at all the options as his stomach growled in anticipation. "Cheese burger and fries, please," he replied.

"That sounds good. I think I'll have the same. How about an apple pie for dessert?" Carter asked.

Jose's eyes lit up.

Carter wanted Jose to trust him and open up to him about what he had witnessed. "My Mom took me to McDonald's once as a reward for making straight A's on my report card. I can still remember the happy meal she bought for me. It had a surprise toy, the Star Wars character Chewbacca. I was so thrilled. Do you like the Star Wars movies?" Carter asked.

Jose thought for a little while. "I don't think I've seen them."

Carter realized even though Jose looked like a normal American kid, he was far from it. He tried another tactic. "What is your favorite dessert?"

"I love chocolate ice cream with chocolate syrup and whipped topping. When Mama has a day off she sometimes takes me to the tourist part of town where there is a place that makes the best ice cream. She let's me get two scoops."

"That sounds awesome," Rosa said. "Your mom sounds very nice."

Jose suddenly became quiet as if they were talking about someone who was dead. He took the last bite of his apple pie.

"Did you get enough to eat?" Carter asked, amazed that he had finished it all.

"Yes, I'm stuffed," Jose replied.

"Good. Why don't we hit the rest room before being stuck in the car for several hours?" Rosa added.

Carter dumped the food cartons in the garbage then followed Jose inside the rest room. He wasn't going to let Jose out of his sight. He didn't want to give him another opportunity to escape. Carter washed his hands at the basin and Jose followed suit. "Ready to hit the road buddy?"

"Where're you taking me?" Jose asked with concern in his voice.

"I'm going to take you back to Miami and try to make arrangements to reunite you with your mom."

Jose seemed satisfied with that answer and followed Carter back to his Mustang.

"This sure is a fancy car. How fast will it go?" Jose asked as they got on their way.

"It can outrun most criminals," Carter said with a smile. He wanted to keep Jose talking. "Do you have any pets?"

"No, I don't have a pet unless you count the lizards I play with in the yard sometimes. I always wanted a dog but Mama said they cost too much."

"I have a pet macaw named Rosco. He is quite a talker. Being from Belize, I bet you see plenty of beautiful birds?"

"The macaws are so noisy in the trees around the sugarcane fields. Do you keep Rosco in a cage?"

"Rosco has a very large cage. But I open the door when I'm home so he can fly around the room. I bet Rosco would like to meet you."

Jose didn't respond. He was thinking about home.

Reading Jose's mind, Carter asked "I know you must miss your home. Why don't you tell me about it? What's your typical day like?"

Jose hesitated, remembering his last day in Belize. "Mama wakes me up early each morning while it's still dark. I have to hurry to get to the sugarcane field by daybreak or someone else will take my job. My uncle drives me, along with several other boys."

"Do you go to school?"

"Not during the summer. The sugarcane harvest is almost complete and school will be starting again soon."

Carter felt sorry for the hard life the boy was forced to live. "What does your mother do for a living?"

"She works as a maid. Nana also lives with us and helps around the house while Mama is working."

Carter tried to steer the conversation in a different direction to get some answers about the murder. "Do you live close to the airport?"

"Yes, I like watching the airplanes fly over our house at night."

"How did you get into the airplane without being spotted?"

"An animal had dug a hole under the fence surrounding the airport. I was able to squeeze through the opening and walk to the airplane without being seen."

"How did you get on the airplane without anyone catching you?" Carter pursued.

"There were two men arguing. While they weren't paying attention I slipped inside."

"So once inside the cargo area you hid behind a crate?"

"Yes."

"What happened after that?" Carter eagerly asked.

"I got cold and found a suitcase big enough for me to fit inside of to stay warm."

Carter made eye contact with Rosa to show his disappointment. Rosa tried a different approach. "After you hid behind the crate could you still hear the men arguing?"

"Yes."

"Can you tell me what they were arguing about?"

"One man said something about getting caught and he needed to stop something. The other man told him to calm down and finish loading the bags."

"Is that all you could hear?"

Jose thought back to the noise he had heard. The loud thump and gurgling noise he tried to forget.

Carter spoke up, "Don't be scared. I won't let anyone hurt you."

"The arguing stopped and I peeked around the crate. One of the men took out a knife and stabbed the other man in the neck. I dove back behind the crate and stayed there until the plane was in the air."

"That must've been horrible to witness," Rosa spoke up.

"Could you identify the man with the knife, if you saw him again?" Carter continued to probe.

"Yes."

Carter waited to see if Jose added anything else. "Jose, did you know the man with the knife?"

"Yes, it was my uncle."

Six

They arrived in Miami just as the sun slipped below the horizon, around nine. Carter knew if he took Jose to the police department, family services and immigration would be contacted. He needed to keep Jose safe until his uncle could be apprehended. Carter dropped Rosa off at the precinct so she could pick up her car, and then took Jose home with him.

Carter opened the door to his apartment and Jose heard, "Bang, bang, get on the ground!"

"Hello, Rosco. It's just me," Carter announced.

"Hello," Rosco squawked back.

"Jose, I'd like you to meet Rosco. He was confiscated from a boat that was raided by police. I think it may have traumatized him. Any time someone enters the apartment the first thing that comes out of his beak is *Bang, bang, get on the ground*. He's just repeating what he heard the police do and say."

Jose smiled and approached the bird cage in the corner of the room. "You must be lonely in here all by yourself."

"I had someone check on him while I was away."

"Rosco need food," the Macaw spoke up.

"Your dish is full of food," Carter replied as he opened the door to Rosco's cage.

Rosco immediately climbed to the top of his cage and stood on his perch so he was at eye level with Carter.

Carter continued to talk with Rosco as if he were human. Rosco finally persuaded Carter to give him some fresh food and water.

Jose laughed as he watched the exchange of words.

Carter smiled, realizing that this was the first time he had heard Jose laugh. "How about I order us a pizza for supper? What do you like on your pizza?"

"I like cheese."

"Good, then one large pizza with extra cheese it is."

The pizza arrived and Jose devoured three pieces without slowing down. "We've had another long day. After you finish eating, it is time to clean up and get ready for bed. I placed your new clothes in the guest room along with the pajamas we bought today."

Jose washed down his pizza with a can of soda. He helped Carter pick up the dirty utensils and placed them in the sink. Then he threw away his paper plate without having to be asked.

Someone has taught Jose good manners, Carter thought to himself. He watched as Jose disappeared into the bathroom. He heard the water running when the phone rang. It was his captain asking for a status report. He reluctantly shared that Jose was staying with him for the night. He relayed that Jose identified his uncle as the person who murdered the man in the airplane. There would also be drug charges pending against him after what Carter witnessed in Orlando. The captain made it very clear that now that Jose had given his statement he needed to be returned to his family in Belize.

Before Carter could protest, the captain said, "Good night."

Carter could no longer hear the water running in the bathroom so he opened the door to the guest room to check on Jose. He was sitting on the bed with a troubled look on his face. "Is everything all right?" Carter asked.

"What's going to happen to me tomorrow?"

He must have overheard the conversation with the captain, Carter thought to himself. "Once I determine you're safe, travel arrangements will be made to return you to Belize. You have nothing to worry about tonight. Nothing will happen to you here. I'll take care of everything tomorrow." Carter waited for Jose to crawl underneath the sheets. "I'm right next door if you need anything."

Jose laid in the dark thinking about home and worrying about his mama. What will my uncle do to me when he discovers I told the police about him? Jose wondered as he drifted off to sleep with thoughts of returning home.

Carter went to bed once he was sure Jose was asleep. He removed his gun from his holster that was strapped to his chest. He securely placed it in the gun case in his night stand. He ran his hands through his hair, exhausted after the last few days. He needed to come up with a way to keep Jose in Miami until his uncle was captured. He tossed and turned for awhile with the events from the last two days running through his head. He eventually fell into a restless sleep.

Carter woke to Rosco squawking, "Bang, bang, get on the floor."

Carter immediately retrieved his gun from the nightstand and listened for an intruder. He heard the creak of the guest bedroom door as it opened. He quietly got out of bed, raising his gun in front of him. He opened the door and quickly surveyed the kitchen and living room to make sure it was clear. He didn't want to get jumped from behind. They were empty. He heard a noise coming from Jose's bedroom. He pushed open the bedroom door and yelled, "Freeze or I will blow your brains out!"

"I wouldn't do that or I'll kill Jose."

The gunman held Jose against his chest with the gun pointed at his head. Jose didn't move or make a sound.

"You would kill your own nephew?" Carter took a chance that he was Jose's uncle.

He seemed surprised that Carter knew who he was. "Jose is coming with me. So unless you want him to die, you need to put down your gun, and let me leave."

Carter quickly ran through the different possible shooting scenarios and many didn't end well for Jose. "All right, just relax." Carter reluctantly set his gun on the floor.

Jose's uncle continued to hold Jose tightly against his chest as he slowly walked out of the room. "Don't try to follow me or the kid dies."

51

The door to the apartment closed. Carter immediately retrieved his gun from the floor and ran out the door. They were already out of sight. Carter looked down and realized he wasn't wearing any pants. He ran back inside and quickly slipped on his jeans that were lying on the bedroom floor. He rushed out the door shirtless to the parking lot. He arrived just in time to see the tail light of a black SUV racing away. He hurriedly started his Mustang and squealed his tires, racing to catch up with the SUV. He sped through the red light with little traffic at this time of the morning. He saw the SUV turn right just up ahead. His tires hugged the road as he turned sharply. Then he slowed down. The SUV was gone. He urgently looked for any signs of the vehicle as he drove down the street. He pounded his fist against the steering wheel out of frustration, realizing he had lost Jose again.

***

Jose struggled to get away from his abductor by kicking and biting his arm. He was thrown into the back of the black SUV and the door slammed shut once again. Jose reached for the door handle to escape but it was locked. He was grabbed by the arm forcefully.

"Stop!" Uncle Marcus yelled. "I'm not going to hurt you."

"What do you want from me?" Jose asked, out of breath.

"I'm just trying to protect you. You have no idea what you've gotten yourself into, kid. Now sit tight. Teo is going to take us someplace safe."

The SUV was driven for a short distance when it quickly pulled into an underground garage and abruptly stopped.

"Come with me and don't try to get away," Uncle Marcus said firmly.

Jose was led by the arm to the elevator. They stopped on the third floor and stepped into a deserted hallway. They walked down a short distance and stopped at the door with the numbers 327 on it. Uncle Teo unlocked the door and pushed Jose inside.

"Have a seat on the sofa!" Uncle Teo ordered. "I need to talk to Marcus."

Jose could see the resemblance between Uncle Marcus and Uncle Teo. Uncle Teo was about the same height and build with jet black, curly hair. He watched as they disappeared into the kitchen. He listened intently to hear what was being discussed. He could hear his name being spoken and something about a money exchange at the marina. The kitchen door opened and Uncle Teo reappeared with a forced smile on his face.

Uncle Teo, now calmer, spoke softly. "This is my place. You'll be safe here. I'm going to lock you in the bedroom so you don't get any crazy ideas about running away again. Just relax and get some sleep. Marcus and I have some business to attend to and then we'll be back by the time you wake up. Understand?"

Jose nodded in acknowledgment. He followed Uncle Marcus to the bedroom. "Don't worry Jose, I won't let anything happen to you. Try to get some sleep and I will return shortly."

Jose sat on the bed and watched as his uncle left the room. The door closed behind him. He heard the door being locked so he couldn't escape. The room was sparsely furnished with just a bed. He walked to the window. It was still dark outside. He could see the tail lights of the cars from the street below. The room had a connecting bathroom but no door other than the one in the bedroom. There appeared to be no way out. He had so many questions going through his head. Jose whispered to himself, "Who should I trust? My uncle says he is trying to protect me and keep me safe but the police say the same thing." He didn't have the answers. He was too tired to try to figure it out. He climbed into bed and stared at the ceiling as he strained his ears to listen to the noises in the dark. It was quiet other than the sound of the air conditioner blowing cool air through the vents. He closed his eyes, thinking how much he wished he had never left home, as he drifted off to sleep.

"I lost him!" Carter screamed into his phone at Rosa.

"Calm down and tell me what happened."

Carter relayed the events of the last thirty minutes.

"Okay, we know the SUV license plate number so I'm sure it will be just a matter of time before it shows up. There are only so many places he can hide in Miami."

"I'll be at your place in ten minutes to pick you up," Carter said, trying to regain control of his emotions. He could always count on Rosa to back him up no matter what time of day or night.

As Carter raced through the streets to Rosa's apartment, he ran through the events leading up to Jose's kidnapping. He rationalized his thoughts out loud, "How did they know where Jose was staying? The captain and Rosa were the only ones who knew I had Jose at my place. Did I forget to lock the door? I always lock the door behind me out of habit. Could my apartment have been under surveillance? No way, I looked around the parking lot when we arrived and there was no black SUV in sight." Carter answered his own questions.

Carter pulled up to the curb at Rosa's apartment complex. She walked out of the stairwell with her long, curly, dark hair pulled back, wearing a black t-shirt, and tight jeans. She always looked like she was ready to kill.

"What is our plan?" Rosa asked as she clicked her seatbelt.

"I'm starting to think there's a mole on the police force. The only person other than you that knew Jose was staying at my place was the captain."

"You talked to the captain?"

"Yes, it was around ten."

"Do you think he's our mole?"

"That is unlikely, but maybe his office is bugged. To be on the safe side, we relay as little information as possible to the captain until Jose is found and returned safely."

"There is already a BOLO for the black SUV from when Angelia was shot in Orlando. It is strange the same black SUV was able to make it all the way back to Miami without being spotted by a single police officer. Do you think they changed license plates?"

"I wasn't close enough tonight to see if the plate was the same." Carter replied. "I've an idea. How about I try to contact Chappy, our undercover drug enforcement officer? I'll be careful what I say so as not to blow his cover. He may know the location where Jose is being held."

Chappy answered half asleep. "Can you talk?" Carter asked.

"Yeah, all is good man," he replied quietly.

"Can you tell me what you've discovered on the jelly bean drug ring and who may be behind it? Jose was kidnapped and I think it may have something to do with the drug ring."

"Who is it, babe?" Carter heard on the other end of the phone. "Go back to sleep, just someone needing a fix."

Chappy lowered his voice, "A yacht anchored in the marina is going down this morning at 7AM. Don't blow it for us."

"Understand. I'll stay out of your way."

The call ended. Carter looked at his watch and then at Rosa. It was 5AM. "We have two hours to try to find Jose. A yacht is being raided in the marina and I pray Jose isn't being held on the boat."

***

Carter searched what seemed like every street in Miami for any sign of the black SUV. The vehicle seemed to have vanished and was nowhere in sight. The glow on the horizon indicated sunrise was not far away. Carter rubbed the exhaustion from his eyes.

"Don't worry, we'll find him." Rosa could sense Carter's frustration.

"We'd better head over to the marina so we can be in place before the raid," Carter said with a bit of apprehension.

Carter pulled into the marina parking lot. The lot was almost empty at this hour. All seemed quiet. He parked by a waterfront restaurant which provided him and Rosa a good view of the boats anchored at the marina. The restaurant was just starting to show signs of activity as patrons arrived for breakfast. Carter rolled down his window and inhaled the fresh, humid morning air. The docks were quiet other than the sound of lines clinking against the mast of the sailboats staying at the marina. Carter waited impatiently as seven o'clock approached.

He became alert as he spotted a couple of fishermen, pulling a cart with fishing supplies, walking down the dock toward the yacht parked at the end. The fishermen were followed by a man and a women dressed in tourist tropical attire.

"It's going down," Carter whispered. They watched intently, ready to draw their weapons and help if needed.

There was no sign of anyone on the deck of the yacht. The fishermen reached into their cart and pulled out two shotguns. They quietly made their way on deck. Carter couldn't stand by and wait any longer to see what happened next. He jumped out of his Mustang and Rosa followed. That's when they heard the first shot explode into the early morning. They took off running down the dock with their guns drawn. By the time they reached the yacht two more shots rang out. Carter jumped aboard the boat with his badge clearly displayed around his neck. He didn't want to be mistaken for a drug dealer. He looked around and entered the salon area. There were two bodies lying facedown on the ground. The two cops pretending to be tourists stood over them with guns drawn while they checked for a pulse.

Carter held up his badge for the officers to see. Carter introduced himself and explained, "I'm trying to find a boy that was kidnapped last night."

One of the cops dressed as a fisherman came up from below. "You won't believe what I found."

Carter and Rosa followed the officer. When they stepped into the small back bedroom they were caught off guard at what they saw. They had expected to find drugs, but instead the terrified look on the faces of eight kids stared back at them. They looked into the sunken pale eyes of the children who couldn't be more than twelve years old. Carter quickly searched the faces for Jose's. There were three boys and five girls bound and gagged. Carter breathed a sigh of relief at not finding Jose.

Rosa immediately took over the role as mother and consoled the children. "It's all right. We're police officers. You have nothing to fear." She repeated in Spanish as she started to remove the gags and gently untie their bound wrists. She searched their bodies for any wounds but didn't find any external injuries. They appeared to be drugged and traumatized. None of them spoke a word or responded to Rosa's touch. She stayed with the children until the emergency personnel arrived, letting them know they were safe.

Carter returned to the upper deck and helped assist the drug enforcement officers in securing the scene. He leaned over the two bodies lying facedown on the deck. "I might know one of the men. Do you mind if I turn him over to get a better look?"

"I don't want the bodies moved until the CSI unit arrives. Just lift their heads so you can see their faces."

Carter did as instructed and pulled the head up by the hair. It was what he feared. Jose's uncle's face stared back at him. With him dead, how was he going to locate where Jose was being held?

"This man kidnapped a boy tonight. He was also my prime suspect in a murder that occurred in the cargo area of an airplane from Belize a few days ago, and he shot a nun in Orlando yesterday."

"That's one criminal I'm glad to see off the streets," the officer dressed in the Hawaiian shirt said.

"He was also the only one who could tell me where he hid the boy he kidnapped."

The boat was suddenly swarming with emergency personnel and officers. The children were brought up from below deck and escorted to the waiting ambulances. Their emotionless, blank stares were heartbreaking. Carter and Rosa stayed just long enough to give their statement.

The adrenaline of the take down had worn off and Carter was exhausted. They walked back to Carter's Mustang still parked by the restaurant. Carter hesitated before starting the car, looking out over the marina. "We're at another dead-end. Where do we start looking for Jose now that his uncle is dead?" he asked Rosa.

Rosa sat quietly for a minute, at a loss for words after what she had witnessed. "We can only hope that his uncle hid him somewhere safe before leaving for the yacht. Jose is a fighter and if there is any way to escape he will find it. Don't worry, we'll locate him." Rosa tried to reassure Carter.

Seven

Jose woke to a room full of sunlight. He slowly remembered the events of the previous night. He looked around the bedroom and up at the ceiling. He wondered what to do about his predicament. He remembered his uncle's words, "*I'm just trying to protect you. You have no idea what you've gotten yourself into.*"

What did my uncle mean? Was he really just trying to protect me? Should I just stay put until he returns or try to escape again? These questions ran through his mind.

As the morning turned into noon Jose started to doubt his uncle was going to return. He was thirsty and hungry. Jose tried the door again, hoping that while he slept it had been unlocked. The handle didn't budge. He went into the bathroom, turned on the faucet and splashed water on his face, then drank from the faucets using his hands. He looked around the bedroom again trying to find anything he could use to escape. He pushed with all his strength against the window pane trying to open the window, but it wouldn't budge. He inspected the door and came up with an idea. He needed to find something to remove the pins from the door jamb. The blinds had a sturdy plastic rod that was used to open and close the blinds. He climbed on a chair and unhooked the rod from the top of the blinds. It was about the same diameter as the door jamb pins. Next, he searched the closet for something he could use as a hammer. On the shelf above the clothes rod he spied a block of wood. He pushed the chair over, climbed on the seat, and stood on his tiptoes but couldn't quite reach the wood. He grabbed an empty coat hanger and used it to hook the edge of the wood. He slowly slid the object toward him until it was in reach. The block of wood was about the size of his foot. It was just the right size for him to hold in his hand. He pushed the plastic rod against the pin in the door jamb and gently tapped it with the block of wood. He was thrilled when it started to move. He slowly knocked the pin out of the door jamb until it was loose enough to grab with his hand and remove it. Only three more pins to go.

By the time he removed the last pin, blisters had formed on his hands. He used the coat hanger and jammed it between the molding and the door hinge to break the door free. He leaped out of the way as the door came crashing down. It hit the carpeted floor with a muffled bang. Jose climbed over the door. He quickly looked around the apartment to confirm he was still alone. The place was empty. "Now what? Should I listen to my Uncle and wait for him to return?" Jose asked himself.

Jose's stomach ached from hunger. He opened the refrigerator and found it empty except for one piece of leftover pizza. He smelled the pizza and decided it was safe to eat. He made himself comfortable on the sofa and slowly ate the cold, tough pizza. He couldn't reach the glasses above the kitchen counter so he stuck his head under the faucet and drank some more water. He thought about leaving but didn't like the idea of spending the night on the street unprotected. He was still in the pajamas that Carter had given him, with no shoes. He walked into the other bedroom to search for clothes and shoes he could wear. The few clothes that hung in the closet were way too big for him and he couldn't find any shoes.

Full from the pizza and tired from the energy he exerted to remove the door, he walked back to the sofa and found the TV remote. He flipped through the channels and stopped at an animated movie. He laughed as he watched the characters dancing around the screen until the noise lulled him to sleep.

He woke with a start at the sound of the door being opened.

"How did you get out?"

"I got hungry."

"Here, put on these clothes and shoes. We need to get going."

Jose grabbed the clothes that were thrown at him and hurriedly dressed. "Where is my Uncle?"

"He was detained and asked me to take care of you. You aren't safe here any longer. We need to get moving."

"Are you going to take me home?"

"No kid. I'm not taking you home." Jose was shoved out the door and dragged by his arm to the parking lot. The man opened the back door of an older model four door sedan. Jose was ordered, "Get in and lie down on the seat so no one sees you. If you try anything I'll place you in the trunk."

Jose obeyed and spread out across the back seat. The car started and Jose heard the doors lock. He laid there motionless, wondering where he was being taken.

✳✳✳

Carter drove away from the marina with no specific destination in mind. It was now way past time for lunch. He was still upset that he had lost his only lead to possibly finding where Jose had been taken.

Rosa broke the silence in the car, "I'm starved. How about we stop for a bite to eat? Once we get re-energized maybe we can come up with a plan."

Carter couldn't argue. Even though he didn't have much of an appetite he knew he needed some food and caffeine. He pulled into the next fast food restaurant. They ordered and found a table by the windows facing the door. That way Carter could keep an eye on anyone entering the restaurant. He always felt safer when he could see when trouble was approaching.

In between bites of french fries Rosa went over what little they knew. "We know the license plate number to the black SUV Jose's uncle was driving is registered to a dummy corporation. Why don't we search the property appraiser's web site and see if there is any more property registered under that name? If we can, then maybe we'll find Jose."

"You know, you may just have something," Carter said. He shoved the last bit of his burger into his mouth. "Let's hurry. Take the rest of your food to go. Once it's discovered that Jose's uncle is dead they may try to move Jose to another location."

Eight

Jose felt the car come to a sudden stop. The driver turned off the engine. Jose laid still in the back seat as ordered. "Come with me!" the man yelled. The passenger door flew open and Jose was pulled by the arm from the back seat.

Jose looked around. He was in a neighborhood full of small wood frame houses stacked one beside the other. He followed the man inside the house and was met by a plump woman that looked to be about the same age as his mother.

"What do we have here? Have you brought home another stray?"

"Juanita, this is Jose. Can you keep an eye on him for a day or two until I have time to straighten things out?"

"What've you gotten yourself into now? Where is his mother?"

"I don't have time to explain. Just let him stay here for a day or two and I'll be back to pick him up."

"All right, but you better come back for him. I don't want to get in any trouble with immigration."

The man drove away and Jose stood there, not sure what to do next. Juanita lifted his face in her hands. "What is your story?" She didn't wait for a response. "Are you hungry?"

Jose shook his head no. He was still full from the pizza he had eaten at the apartment.

"I have things I need to do around the house. Why don't you go out back and play with the other kids?"

Juanita lead Jose to a small fenced in back yard. There were five other boys who looked younger than him. A rickety wooden fence surrounded the backyard. The white paint used to protect the wood was flaking off and the wood was rotting near the ground. There were weeds growing everywhere, with some sand in between. There was a rusted swing set and plastic slide the kids were playing on in the summer heat. A hot wind blew, providing little relief. Jose sat on the ground in the shade of the house and watched while the other children played. He tried to decide whether he should try to leave or stay. He couldn't see over the wooden fence, but could hear dogs barking on the other side. As the sun grew low in the horizon, three of the boys left with another woman that Jose figured must have been their mother.

Jose was told to clean up for supper. He sat quietly with the three family members and enjoyed the beans, rice, and tortillas. After supper Juanita bathed and put the remaining two boys to bed while Jose sat on the sofa and watched TV.

Juanita appeared with a pillow, sheet, and blanket. "Get up so I can make your bed."

Jose obeyed and stood up. He watched as she placed the sheet over the worn sofa.

"It's late, and time to get some sleep. You should be comfortable enough in here," Juanita said as she turned off the TV and lights.

Jose slipped underneath the blanket and laid in the dark unable to sleep. He missed his mother. He could hear the sounds of traffic and loud music in the distance. He felt more alone now than he ever had. His thoughts wandered to Carter. Was he looking for him? He laid there trying to come up with a plan to get out of the mess he had gotten himself into. Then he heard a jet fly low overhead. He remembered seeing the airplanes flying overhead earlier in the day while in the back yard. There must be an airport close by, he thought to himself. If he could get to the airport maybe he could find his way back home. Jose drifted off to sleep after deciding he would slip away tomorrow morning before the man returned.

***

Carter and Rosa hurriedly performed a property search for GFH Corporation. There were two properties listed. One was located on the beach and one just a few blocks from Carter's place. "That has to be where they took him." Carter pointed to the address closest to his place.

"That's why I lost sight of the SUV so fast. They must've turned into a parking garage before I could catch up with them." Carter scribbled down the address. "Lets take my car, it's faster."

"What makes you think that my Dodge Dart can't keep up with your car?" Rosa laughed.

"Maybe the fact that it goes from zero to sixty in thirty minutes," Carter said.

"Hey, it's not that bad. It has been a very reliable little car."

Carter weaved in and out of traffic. He hoped he would find Jose safe and still alive. Carter hadn't been to church in a while but he was raised Catholic. He said a silent prayer under his breath and asked God to help him locate Jose before it was too late.

Carter came to a screeching stop in front of the apartment building. He didn't wait for the elevator. He found the stairwell and ran up the three flights of stairs, taking two steps at a time. He stopped when he reached apartment 327.

"How do you want to handle this?" Rosa asked quietly? "Do we knock or go with the element of surprise?"

Carter tried the door and it was unlocked. He whispered back, "Element of surprise."

They both drew their weapons, slowly opening the door. Carter pointed for Rosa to search to the left while he went right. Carter came to a stop in front of the bedroom where the door laid on the floor.

Carter heard Rosa yell, "Clear!"

Carter yelled back, "Jose was here."

Rosa walked into the bedroom and Carter held up the pajamas Jose was wearing before he was kidnapped from his place. "We're too late once again," Carter said, frustrated.

"Wait a minute, not so fast. It looks like he may have escaped on his own." Rosa reached down and picked up the wood block Jose had used as a hammer.

"Where does that leave us? If he did escape, where's he hiding or did they capture him again before he could get away?"

"Think about it. Jose's uncle grabs Jose and takes him to this apartment. But he has unfinished business and locks Jose in the bedroom so he can't escape while he's gone. Jose's uncle is killed on the yacht before he can return to the apartment to retrieve him. Jose manages to free himself and leaves, not knowing that his uncle is dead."

"Okay, that's a definite possibility based on what we see around us. But where does that leave us? We still have no idea where Jose may be."

Carter and Rosa searched the apartment for any other clues. "This place looks hardly lived in. It definitely wasn't being used as a permanent residence for anyone," Carter said.

"Now what?" Rosa asked.

"I'm not sure." Carter closed the door on their way out. He drove them back to the station in silence. Rosa had been around Carter long enough to know when to keep quiet and just let him think.

Rosa broke the silence first. "It has been a long day. Why don't you go home and get some rest? We'll start fresh again in the morning when we both can think more clearly."

Carter hated to admit defeat, but he knew Rosa was right. He was exhausted and could hardly concentrate anymore. He had this horrible sick feeling though, that time was running out.

***

Jose woke to the sounds of dishes clanging together in the kitchen. It was still dark outside but he figured sunrise must not be far away. He had slept in the clothes he had arrived in. He got up

66

from the sofa, put on his tennis shoes, and wandered into the kitchen.

"Good morning. Were you able to sleep on that lumpy sofa?" Juanita cheerfully asked.

Jose nodded yes.

"Would you like a bowl of cereal while I wake up my boys?"

Before he could answer she set a bowl on the table along with a large box of Cheerios and milk. He helped himself while she disappeared into the other room. He hurriedly ate the cereal and waited for the right time to slip away. Juanita returned with her two boys in tow and busied herself with feeding them. The three boys that were there yesterday showed up a short time later, being dropped off by their mother.

"You boys go outside to play while I clean up the kitchen and start some laundry."

Jose followed the boys outside. He watched as one played in the sand with a plastic dump truck while the others slid down the slide. He decided this was his chance. He noticed one of the boards was loose on the fence surrounding the back yard. He lifted the board and saw it opened to the neighbors yard, but there was a path to the street. It was tight but he managed to wiggle his slender body through the opening. He pushed the board back in place and quickly walked away.

The street was congested with cars. He knew he needed to get out of sight as fast as he could before Juanita discovered he was gone. An airplane roared overhead. That was the sign he needed to guide him in the direction of the airport. He cut across an alley and feared for his life as snarling dogs growled at him from the other side of a fenced yard. He quickly ran past the house. The end of the alley led to a street with many run-down businesses. There were boards or bars across all the windows. Then he saw the perfect place to hide. There was an old small white wooden church at the end of the street. He thought of Angelia and wondered how she was doing after being shot trying to protect him. He felt bad for all the trouble he had caused her.

Concrete steps led to the entrance of the church. He cautiously opened the door and didn't see anyone. The church reminded him of the one his mama used to take him to sometimes. It was always bustling with activity on Sunday mornings. Sometimes after the church service there would be a pot luck lunch where everyone brought their favorite dishes. There would always be a delicious variety of food to choose from. He quietly entered the church and looked around inside. He still didn't see anyone. He sneaked inside the confessional before anyone saw him. He could hear voices in the distance toward the front of the sanctuary. He hoped he could remain hidden long enough until he was sure it was safe to leave. That plan was quickly spoiled when the door to the confessional opened.

"Well hello there, young man. My name is Father Benito. Have you come to confess your sins today?" The father smiled down at Jose's little body curled up with his knees against his chest.

Jose was at a loss for words and didn't know how to respond to the Father's question.

"You look like you could use something to drink. Sister Catherine has just made some fresh lemonade in the kitchen. Would you like a glass?"

Jose had never had lemonade but was very thirsty from his walk. "Yes, please," he responded.

Father Benito lead Jose to the kitchen. "Look who I found hiding in the confessional. Can you spare a glass of lemonade for this young man?"

Sister Catherine smiled, "I think I can manage that."

Jose took the class offered to him and drank greedily.

"Slow down there son or you will get a brain freeze," Father Benito laughed.

"What is that?" Jose uttered.

"That's when you drink something ice cold too fast and you give yourself a headache."

Jose thought that sounded strange but drank the rest of his lemonade slower just in case the priest was right. He handed his empty glass to Sister Catherine. "Thank you. I better get going."

"Where are you headed in such a hurry? We serve lunch in about an hour. You don't want to miss Sister Catherine's ham and bean soup with corn bread. I guarantee it will be the best you've ever tasted. I think she has also made chocolate cake for dessert. If you're like most boys I know, you will love it."

That did sound awfully good. Jose didn't know when he would get a chance to eat again. "Okay, I guess I could stay a little longer."

"Good. If you aren't too busy I sure could use some help putting together a bookshelf in my office."

Jose followed Father Benito down the hall toward the back of the church. They entered a small room. On the floor was a bookshelf that had seen better days.

"All we need to do is put in a few nails to hold the shelves in place. Then we will give it a fresh coat of paint. It'll look as good as new."

Jose was skeptical that the bookshelf would look like new when finished, but was eager to help. He held the boards while Father Benito securely nailed them in place. Then Father Benito placed a plastic cloth on the floor and set the bookshelf on the plastic. He handed Jose a paintbrush and opened a can of brown paint. "All you have to do is dip your brush like this in the can, wipe off the excess so it doesn't drip, and then slowly move the brush across the surface of the boards. Now you try."

Jose did as instructed. He dipped the brush in the paint and slowly lifted it wiping the excess off on the edge of the can. Then he brushed the paint on the wood surface starting with the top shelf. He was careful not to make a mess.

While they worked together covering the bare wood with paint, Father Benito slowly pried information from Jose by asking him questions. What the Father didn't realize, though, was that Jose was making up his answers.

"Do you live around here?"

"Yes, I just moved to the area."

"That's wonderful! We would love to have your family come to our church."

"My mom isn't too religious."

"It would be a great way for you to meet some new people in town."

"My dad works on the police force." Jose didn't know why he blurted that out.

"Is that right? What's his name? I know many of the officers that work in the area. Maybe I've met him."

"His name is Carter, but I don't think you'd know him since we just moved here," Jose rationalized.

"Maybe when we're finished painting I can give him a call. He can join us for lunch then take you home."

"I don't know his phone number."

"Well, that's all right. We can meet another time. You're doing a great job. Keep painting and I'll be right back. Then we can stop for lunch."

Father Benito returned a short time later and took Jose to the fellowship area. There were tables lined in rows filling every inch of the room. A steady stream of people were arriving for lunch. Jose was escorted to a chair next to Sister Catherine. She placed a big bowl of ham and bean soup along with a piece of corn bread in front of Jose. Everyone bowed their heads while Father Benito blessed the meal.

Jose took a big spoonful of soup and crammed it in his mouth. He had never tasted anything so good, at least that is until dessert. Sister Catherine cut him a big piece of chocolate cake and placed it in front of him. Jose savored the sweet chocolate treat. He thought his stomach might explode by the time he ate the last bite. The room was full of chatter as everyone enjoyed their meal. Jose had forgotten about his predicament while he listened to Sister Catherine tell him stories of when she was a child. She got up to help clear the table and that's when Jose's problems suddenly came back to him. He looked up and saw the man that had taken him to Juanita's house. Jose dove under the table before he could be seen. He watched, hidden from view, as the man talked to Father Benito. He didn't want to be caught and knew he had to leave immediately. He stayed low to the ground, hiding below all the tables, and slipped out the back door of the church without being seen.

✱✱✱

Carter and Rosa sat at their desk trying to figure out where to start looking for Jose next. "Carter, you have a call on line 1!" another detective yelled to him.

Hoping it was Jose, Carter hurriedly picked up the phone and pressed 1. "Hello, this is Carter."

"I'm so glad I found you. This is Father Benito. Your son is with me."

Carter almost responded, you must have the wrong number, when he realized he might be talking about Jose. "You have Jose?" he anxiously asked.

"Yes, he showed up here early this morning and I got the impression he didn't want to be found."

Carter didn't know what Jose had told the priest but he played along. "Thank you so much for taking care of him. I hope he wasn't any trouble."

"None at all. He helped me paint a bookshelf while he shared with me about you just moving to the area." Father Benito gave Carter the address for the church.

"Please don't let him out of your sight. I'll leave immediately and should be there in thirty minutes to pick him up."

Carter was elated when he hung up the phone and yelled at Rosa, "Let's go! Jose is at a Catholic church on the west side of town."

Carter filled Rosa in on his conversation with Father Benito on the way to the church. "Why do you think Jose told Father Benito that I was his father?"

"You must have made a connection with him. At least now we know he's safe and not being held captive someplace."

Carter came to a screeching stop in front of the church. He jumped out and raced toward the entrance. He was eager to see for himself that Jose was safe. He made his way through the crowd in the fellowship hall looking for Jose and Father Benito. He saw Father Benito standing toward the back of the room talking to a man that seemed very agitated. Carter hurriedly walked toward Father Benito and heard Jose's name being mentioned. This further peaked Carter's interest. Now he was just a few feet away when the man talking to Father Benito looked up and saw Carter approaching, then took off running out the side door. Carter chased after him. Being in very good shape, it didn't take him long to catch up with the man. He leaped, knocking the man to the ground. Rosa raced up from behind to assist him.

"Cuff him and take him to my car until I can figure out what's going on," Carter said to Rosa as he tried to catch his breath.

Carter went back into the church and found a concerned look on Father Benito's face. "Where is Jose, and how does that man know him?"

"Shortly after I called you, this man came into the church and told me he was looking for his son, Jose. I asked him his name and he said his name was Diego. He explained that his son had run away from home this morning. Well, obviously I thought that was strange, since Jose told me his dad's name was Carter. So I stalled him until you arrived to sort out who the real dad was."

"Where is Jose?"

Father Benito glanced toward the seat where Jose had been sitting. "He was right over there. He may have gone back to my office to finish painting the bookshelf we were working on together."

Carter followed the Father to his office but they found it deserted. After searching the church it was apparent Jose had escaped again.

"He couldn't have gotten far. Not more than fifteen minutes have passed since I last saw him at the table."

"Thanks for your help, Father. If he shows up please don't hesitate to call my cell phone." Carter handed him a card with his number on it before hurrying from the church to try to catch up with Jose.

✳✳✳

Jose ran as fast as he could away from the church. He cut down a side street and saw a large building with children standing in front. As he approached he realized it was a school. Several school buses were parked in front of the building as the children were being loaded. Jose tried to catch his breath and slowly made his way to the back of one of the lines. He walked onto the bus without being questioned. Jose took a seat next to a kid with glasses and a little overweight. The bus started to pull away from the school and Jose breathed a sigh of relief.

The kid next to him spoke up, "Would you like some jelly beans?"

"No! Where did you get those?" Jose asked abruptly.

"An older kid at the school gave them to me."

Jose tried to explain. "My Dad works for the police department and there are some jelly beans that'll make you sick if you eat them. I would throw them out if I were you."

The kid thought about what Jose said and placed the jelly beans back in his backpack. "Are you new? I haven't seen you on this bus before."

"Yeah, my Dad and I just moved to the area. Today was my first day at this school."

"What grade are you in?"

Jose wasn't sure how to answer without letting the boy know he was lying. "I'm not sure where they are going to place me yet. My records from my old school haven't arrived. What grade are you in?"

"I'm in the sixth grade."

The bus stopped and several kids got off.

"What neighborhood do you live in?"

Jose stammered as he tried to come up with an answer. "I get off at the next stop."

"Me too. Do you want to come over to my house and play video games? My dad and stepmom won't be home for another two hours."

Jose thought for a second before answering, "Yeah, that sounds like fun. My Dad won't be home from work for a while either."

They stepped off the bus and Jose followed the boy down the sidewalk. He was mesmerized by the nice homes and well kept yards. It was just like the photographs in the book he had on America. Jose was lost in his dream of living in such a neighborhood when the boy spoke up.

"My nickname is Readley because I'm always reading. But I love playing video games, too."

"I'm Jose."

Jose stepped inside Readley's house and stopped in his tracks. He stared up at the high ceilings and staircase to the second story in front of him. He was wide-eyed with amazement and couldn't image living in a home with so many rooms.

"Follow me. My room is up here."

Jose hesitated before stepping on the nice hardwood floors. He wiped his shoes on the rug at the entrance before proceeding. He climbed to the top of the stairs and entered Booker's bedroom. There was a large bed, desk with a laptop, and a television. Jose thought to himself, if I lived here I would never leave this room.

"Which game do you want to play first?"

"Whichever one you want is fine with me." Jose had never played any video games.

Booker loaded the game and handed Jose a controller. Booker explained the rules and Jose quickly caught on as to how to make the objects move across the screen. He lost the first few games before finally winning one. Two hours had passed before Jose realized it.

GAME OVER popped on the screen. Booker yelled, "I won! Let's go downstairs and get some cookies."

Jose followed Booker into the kitchen.

"You want a Coke?" Booker asked as he opened the refrigerator and took out two cans of soda and handed one to Jose. Then he grabbed a bag of peanut butter cookies. They returned to the bedroom to devour their treats. They sat on the floor, legs crossed, and munched away until all the cookies and soda were gone. Jose was stuffed once again. He figured he better eat while he could. He wasn't sure when his next meal would be.

"My stepmom should be home soon. I better pick up this stuff before she arrives and yells at me." Booker put away the video games and threw away their trash.

Jose realized he needed to leave before Booker's parents showed up and started asking questions. "Thanks for having me. I also need to get home before my Dad shows up and wonders where I am." Jose liked pretending he was like all the other kids with parents.

"Maybe your Dad will let you come over this weekend and we can play some more games."

"I would like that," Jose said as he walked out the front door, knowing he would probably never see Readley again. He looked up and down the street, unsure which direction to head. A brown UPS truck sped past him and stopped two houses down. Jose walked toward the truck. He watched as the driver got out and walked to the front door of the house with a box in his hand. He made a split second decision and jumped into the back of the truck before the driver saw him. He stepped over the few boxes and quickly covered himself with a tarp that was lying in the corner on the floor. He concealed himself so the driver wouldn't notice him. He listened as the engine started and he felt the truck jerk forward as they raced down the road. He stayed perfectly still each time the truck came to a stop so he wouldn't be seen. Then the engine was turned off and didn't start up again. He sat motionless for what seemed like an hour but in actuality was only a few minutes. It was hot under the tarp and he was sweating. He poked his head out to make sure he was alone. Through the front windshield he could tell the sun had started to set and it was getting dark. He listened for any noise. He heard jet engines and knew he must be close to the airport. He tried the door but it was locked. He looked out the front window to try to determine where he was located. He was in a large parking area with many more UPS trucks all around him. He heard another airplane taking off. His heart raced with anticipation at the thought of flying home. He was stuck for now, though, with no way out. He was exhausted from the days' events. Darkness surrounded him with only the streetlights in the parking lot keeping him company. The temperature started to drop and he curled up under the tarp to stay warm. He fell asleep dreaming of being home.

***

"Can you believe that we lost him again?" Carter asked frustrated as they returned to the police station.

"Really. We lost him!" Rosa said sarcastically. She turned around and looked at the guy in the back seat. "Maybe he can help shed some light on what's going on."

Carter led the suspect to the interrogation room. Carter spoke first. "Is the name you gave the priest really your name?"

"Yeah, my name is Diego. I don't know what you think I did, but I didn't do it."

"That's what they all say," Rosa spoke up.

76

"We currently have you on kidnapping charges but if you help us locate Jose, maybe I can get the DA to cut you a break."

"Hey, I didn't kidnap anyone! I was just looking after Jose for a friend when the kid ran away."

"And who might that friend be?" Rosa asked.

"Jose's Uncle Marcus asked me to keep an eye on him until he returned."

"When was the last time you spoke to Marcus?" Carter asked, even though he knew Marcus was dead.

"Early yesterday morning. He said he had an errand to run. He asked me to keep an eye on Jose for a day or so until he returned. When I got off work I picked him up and took him to my sister's house."

"Where's your sister's house so we can confirm your story?" Rosa asked.

"I would rather not say. My sister wouldn't be too happy if I sent cops to her home. She's a very private person."

"Or maybe she might have some problems with immigration?" Rosa added.

"She's a good person and I don't want to cause her any trouble."

Carter decided finding Diego's sister could wait, and took a different approach. "We have traffic camera footage showing you driving the black SUV that abducted Jose." Carter was bluffing. They didn't have a clear image of who was driving the SUV. He just wanted to see if Diego took the bait.

"Hey, you got the wrong guy! I didn't kidnap anyone. I was just doing a friend a favor by looking after his nephew."

"The kid was in police custody when he was taken unwillingly," Carter added.

"That's not on me, man. Marcus just asked me to pick up his nephew and keep an eye on him until he returned. That's all."

Carter could tell Diego was getting nervous. "Maybe if you share what you planned to do with a boat full of girls being held against their will on the docks we can cut a deal."

"I don't know anything about any girls."

"Okay, then what do you know about jelly beans laced with drugs being flown from Belize?"

"I don't know what you're talking about."

"It sounds like you're going to rot behind bars for a very long time for kidnapping if you don't start cooperating," Rosa spoke up.

"All I know is Marcus called and asked for my help in taking care of his nephew. So I helped. That's all I know."

Carter could see he was getting nowhere. "Maybe a few nights in jail will rattle your memory." Carter got up to leave.

"Wait! What can you do for me if I give you a name?"

"That depends on the name."

"I overheard a conversation about a delivery and a name was mentioned. It might have something to do with the girls you were talking about."

"Okay, I'm listening."

"You can't let anyone know this came from me or I'm dead."

"Just give me the name and if it pans out we can see about witness protection."

"The name is GHF Corporation."

That peaked Carter's interest. He knew GHF Corporation had something to do with all of this but didn't have any names to tie to the dummy corporation. Carter spoke up, "We already know about GHF Corporation, so no deal." He got up to leave once again.

"Wait, wait! The name is Dragone. That is the name I overheard. He has something to do with GHF Corporation."

"As in J. R. Dragone, the real estate tycoon?"

"Yeah, I think that's who they were talking with."

Carter looked at Rosa and smiled. "What exactly did you overhear them say to Dragone?"

"Just that his package was ready for delivery. That's all I heard. Now what can you do for me?"

"If your lead helps solve this case and I find Jose unharmed I'll talk to the DA about dropping the kidnapping charges."

"Hey, wait a minute! I thought you said if I cooperated you would cut me a deal. I can't be held responsible for Jose running away."

Carter and Rosa stood up to leave. Diego shouted vulgarities at them as they left the room.

Rosa spoke up. "Do you believe he was involved in the kidnapping?"

"I'm not sure. Obviously we don't have enough evidence to hold him on kidnapping charges. All we have for now is that he asked Father Benito about Jose who had supposedly run away from his sisters. I just want him to sit in jail for a day to see if he remembers anything else that might help us before we release him."

"Now what? We don't have enough for a warrant on any property that J. R. Dragone owns to determine if he's hiding more girls."

"It's late and I'm exhausted. How about we sleep on it tonight and come up with a new game plan in the morning? Maybe by then Jose will tell someone else to call me again," Carter said.

"At least you know you made an impact on the boy or he never would've told the priest you're his father."

A sad look crossed Carter's face as he worried about Jose's safety. The streets of Miami can be harsh at night. He had seen too many tragic endings to kids who disappeared. "Maybe I will drive through the streets around the church one more time to see if Jose appears."

"Do you want some company?"

"No, get some rest. I'll see you in the morning."

✳✳✳

Jose woke with a start from his hiding place in the back of the UPS truck. The door to the truck opened with a clatter and the truck's engine roared to life. Jose pulled the tarp over his head so he wouldn't be seen. The truck moved only a short distance before stopping and the engine was turned off. Jose slowly emerged from underneath the tarp. He checked to make sure he was alone. It was still dark outside. The driver was nowhere in sight. He crept to the front of the vehicle and hurriedly jumped out the drivers side door before he was seen, then dashed underneath another truck backed up to the loading dock. Jose could hear voices and the noise of the forklifts as they loaded the trucks with freight. He stayed low and hid in the dark shadows of the early morning. The streetlights in the parking lot guided him. He walked briskly away from the loading docks and stopped once he reached the side of the building. He crouched down behind some shrubs to catch his breath, then glanced over the hedge to get his bearings. He was surrounded by a parking lot full of car and UPS trucks. Then he heard a wonderful noise, the roar of an airplane engine as it ramped up to take off. Excited, he jumped up from his hiding place. He was so close to the runway he could see the flashing lights of the airplanes waiting to take off. Now fully awake and loaded with energy, he weaved in and out of the parked cars until he reached the street. He walked down the sidewalk for a short ways when he spotted a large sign. "Airport Parking," he read out loud. He watched as an airport shuttle bus exited the parking lot. He noticed a parking attendant at the entrance taking money as the vehicles left. He waited until the parking attendant was distracted, then quickly ran around the fence and entered the parking lot without being seen. He spotted a group of about ten people standing at the curb by the shuttle bus pick up sign. He waited near the group, hidden from sight beside a car, until the bus pulled up. As the crowd moved to get on the bus he stepped forward and joined a family with two kids so he wouldn't stick out. While everyone was busy loading their bags, Jose stepped on the bus unnoticed and took a seat toward the back of the bus. The bus pulled away from the curb and Jose stared out the window as the landscape rushed by.

After a short time the shuttle bus came to an abrupt stop and the driver yelled, "Delta."

Jose saw the family of four stand up. He followed suit and exited along with them, blending into the crowd as they entered the airport terminal. He was immediately surrounded by people rushing to catch their flights. He moved with the masses, trying to stay out of everyone's way so he wouldn't be trampled. The crowd came to a stop and Jose found himself in a long line. The line moved slowly. He figured if everyone else was waiting in this line he must be in the right place. He tried to see around the people in front of him so he knew where the line ended. He moved a few steps a minute for what seemed like an eternity. He finally approached the end of the line, and realized he was in a security checkpoint line. He started to panic, and frantically looked around, trying to find a way past security without being caught. Now there was only one person between him and the man dressed in the security uniform. He started to get out of line and make a run for it when an alarm sounded. A man in another line started to yell at security when they wouldn't let him proceed. The security guard in Jose's line left his post to help with the situation. Jose saw his chance. While the security guard was distracted, Jose walked through without being noticed. Once past the checkpoint he immediately lost himself in the crowd. He followed the other travelers onto the moving sidewalk. When it ended he continued to walk for what seemed like a mile before arriving at the gates where the airplanes were boarding. He searched for a gate with an airplane headed to Belize. He wandered up and down the long terminal aisle reading the destinations: Atlanta, Cincinnati, Los Angeles, Houston, Denver, Boston, Detroit, New York, and Puerto Rico. Belize was not listed. Jose was tired and hungry. He found a vacant chair and sat down in despair. He wanted so badly to go home. He had to figure out a way to find the right airplane. That's when he noticed a large computer screen high above his head flashing flight numbers, gate locations, arrivals, and destination times. He scanned through the list. Then he saw it. Belize! He searched for the gate number when he heard his name.

"Jose, is that you?"

Jose turned and stared up at Aunt Maria.

Jose jumped up from his seat and was hugged tightly by his aunt. "What're you doing here? Your mom has been worried sick about you."

"I know, I'm so sorry. I was just trying to find an airplane flying to Belize so I could go home. Did you fly all the way here for me?" Jose asked.

"I told your mom I would try to find you while I was here, but the reason I came was to take your uncle's body home."

"What do you mean? I saw Uncle Marcus two days ago. He let me stay in an apartment. But he never returned."

"Marcus called to let me know he had found you. He was planning to bring you home. But," she hesitated before she continued. "Jose, the Belize police came to our house yesterday and told me that the Miami police have Marcus in their morgue. I'm sorry, but they told me Marcus was dead."

"No, he's not dead. I just saw him."

"We were so worried that you might've been with him when he was killed. Your mom will be so glad to hear you have been found safe. I know you have a lot explaining to do, but let's get out of the airport first. Then we can give your mom a call to let her know you're okay."

Jose stayed closed to Aunt Maria's side as they made their way through the airport. They walked outside and were greeted by the congested noise of vehicles and buses everywhere. They found the right hotel shuttle bus to take them to their destination, then left the chaos of the airport. They arrived at the hotel thirty minutes later. Once checked into their room, Aunt Maria used her cell phone to dial Jose's mom. "Sophia, this is Maria. You'll never guess who I ran into at the airport!"

Jose was handed the phone. "Hi, Mama." Jose had to hold the phone away from his ear; she was so happy to hear from him.

"Jose, I was worried sick about you. Are you all right?"

"Yes, Mama. I'm fine. I have so much to tell you!"

"Why did you run away? Never mind-we'll catch up when you get home. Let me talk to your aunt."

Jose watched Aunt Maria as she listened to his mama. She looked very sad. She said, "We'll see you tomorrow." She ended the call and looked down at Jose. She was tired from her long journey but tried to smile to let Jose know everything was going to be okay. "You look like you could use a bath. Why don't we both get cleaned up, then walk next door to get something to eat? I saw a fast food restaurant on our way in."

Jose hurriedly washed his face and hands so they could go eat. Aunt Maria was quiet on their walk to the restaurant. Once inside, the smell of fried food tantalized Jose's nose. He almost started to drool he was so hungry.

Aunt Maria must have seen the desperation in his eyes and ordered him a large hamburger, fries, and a milkshake.

They found a table by the window and Jose lost himself in his food.

"Jose, where have you been the last several days?"

Jose took a large swallow of his milkshake and swallowed his mouthful of burger before speaking. "I went to Disney World and then I met Detective Carter. He let me sleep at his place. He has a big bird that talks. Then I stayed with Uncle Marcus. When he didn't return, a man picked me up and took me to his sister's house to stay the night. The next day I decided to leave and find the airport." He left out the part of witnessing the man dying in the cargo bay of the airplane, the jelly beans that almost got him killed, watching Sister Angelia get shot, and being kidnapped from Carter's apartment by Uncle Teo.

"This Detective Carter sounds nice. I'm glad you met someone you could trust to keep you safe."

"Do you think I could talk to him before we leave? He might be worried about me."

"Yes, of course. I'd like to meet him myself and thank him for watching out for you." Aunt Maria wiped a tear from her face as she thought about Marcus. She just couldn't believe he was dead. They finished their meal and walked back to the hotel.

All that food made Jose sleepy and Aunt Maria must have sensed Jose's exhaustion. "Why don't you stay here and take a nap while I go down to the station to make arrangements to bring Marcus home? I'll buy you some clean clothes to change into while I'm out."

Jose climbed underneath the crisp clean white sheets of the large soft bed. Aunt Maria tucked him under the covers snuggly like his mother used to. "Promise me you won't open the door for anyone while I'm gone. If you wake up before I return, don't leave this room. Do you understand?" Aunt Maria asked firmly.

"Yes, I promise."

"I should be back in a couple of hours. This is my cell phone number in case you need to call me." She scribbled her number on the pad sitting on the night stand by the telephone. She kissed Jose on the forehead and told him, "Get some rest. I'll be back before you know it." Maria didn't like the idea of leaving Jose alone but knew taking him to the morgue with her to identify Marcus' body wasn't a good idea. She felt he would be safe in the hotel room and he could get some much needed rest while she was gone.

***

Carter arrived at work the next morning after very little sleep. He had driven around the city most of the night hoping to spot Jose. He was finishing his second cup of coffee when Rosa arrived.

"You look like crap. Did you get any sleep last night?"

"Who needs sleep when we have this god awful coffee?" Carter lifted his mug in the air.

Rosa smiled and handed him a large Starbucks Caffe Mocha. "I figured you could use a boost this morning."

84

"Have I ever told you how much I enjoy having you as a partner?"

"Not near enough," Rosa laughed. "So where are we this morning? Have you come up with a plan on how we are going to investigate J. R. Dragone without him finding out?"

"Not exactly. Let's go over what we do know. Jelly beans laced with a very potent drug are being smuggled into Miami from Belize. Jose's uncle was seen by Jose stabbing Julio Sanchez at the Belize airport before showing up in Miami. Then someone believed to be Jose's uncle kidnapped Jose from my place. We connect GHF Corporation with the apartment Jose's uncle was using and the SUV he was driving. We received a tip from Chappy that something is going down on a yacht in the marina, which is where we found the young girls tied up in the galley, but with no drugs present. Then we get a call that Jose is eating lunch at a Catholic church on the west side of town where we capture Diego. Diego confirms GHF Corporation is involved in whatever is going on and he gives us the name J. R. Dragone, the real estate tycoon, as a possible link. Did I miss anything?"

"Nope, that pretty much sums it up. I just have one question. Why would Chappy, who's an undercover drug enforcement officer, give you a tip about a yacht where no drugs were found?"

"Hmm, that's a good question." Before Carter could call Chappy to get an answer, his phone rang. He quickly answered it. "Carter. I'll be right there." He ended the call. "It's our lucky day. Jose's Aunt Maria is in at the front desk. She has come to identity her husband's body. Maybe she can fill in some of our holes."

Carter and Rosa met Aunt Maria in the lobby. "Hello, I'm detective Carter. Can I ask you a few questions before we take you to identify your husband?"

"Did you say your name is Carter?"

"Yes."

"Jose told me you helped him."

"You know where Jose is located?"

"Yes, he's sleeping in my hotel room. I found him at the airport when I arrived this morning."

"I'm not sure you should've left him alone. He may be in danger. Tell me which hotel you are staying at so I can send an officer to stay with him until we arrive."

Maria provided the information he requested and Carter relayed it to the duty officer.

"Can you share with me how my husband died?" Maria asked.

"All I can tell you at this time is he was found on a yacht in the marina. Gunfire was exchanged when the police arrived. A bullet struck your husband and he was killed instantly. Do you know why your husband was in Miami?"

"He had a family situation he needed to take care of, but that's all I know. He said he would be gone for a few days."

"Did he travel to Miami frequently?"

"No, this came out of the blue. He told me he would tell me all about it when he returned home in a couple of days." Maria wiped a tear from her cheek.

"Did he have family that lived in Miami?"

"None that I'm aware of. I wish I could be more help. I would like to know why Marcus was on that yacht myself."

"I won't delay you any longer. Let me take you down to the morgue so we can get back to Jose," Carter said. He realized that she wasn't going to be able to provide him with any additional information in solving this case.

They made their way down to the basement and approached the cold storage room where the dead bodies were kept until being released. Carter explained to the medial examiner which body they were there to see. They waited in the hall for it to be retrieved. The gurney was wheeled over to the viewing window. Maria braced herself as the sheet was removed.

Maria gasped, "That's not my husband! That's his brother, Teo."

Carter couldn't believe what he was hearing. "Are you sure?"

"Yes. Teo received the chain tattoo around the neck when he was in high school as part of a gang ritual. Marcus has had no contact with him for many years. We weren't even sure if he was still alive."

"Is it possible that Teo contacted Marcus and that's why he came to Miami?"

"It's very possible. Marcus always felt responsible for not protecting Teo from the gangs. But once Teo became a gang member there was nothing Marcus could do. He basically disowned his brother and didn't want any part of what he had become. If Teo contacted Marcus and asked for his help, I know Marcus wouldn't have hesitated to try to save his little brother. The same morning he left for Miami Jose went missing. I contacted Marcus on his cell phone that evening hoping he might know where Jose went. He told me not to worry, that he knew where Jose was located. He told me he had to go before I could ask any more questions."

"So he didn't tell you where Jose was?"

"No, he hung up before I could find out. A day later, while I was at work, he called and left me a message. The message said that he had Jose and was bringing him home. That was the last time I heard from him."

"Who notified you that his body was in the morgue?"

"I received a visit from the Belize police. They told me Marcus was dead. I needed to go to Miami to claim his body so it could be returned to Belize for burial. When I asked how he died they provided very little information other than that he was shot. I thought he must have been robbed or something. I knew he had found Jose and was worried he may have also been injured."

At the mention of Jose's name Carter urgently wanted to see him for himself. "I don't know what's going on here, but we need to get to Jose and make sure you are both safe until we figure it out."

Carter drove recklessly to the hotel, weaving in and out of traffic. He came to a screeching stop in front of the hotel lobby.

They hurried to Maria's room. Maria swiped her key card and the door clicked open.

Maria yelled, "Jose, it's Aunt Maria! Are you awake?"

The bed was empty. She frantically looked in the bathroom. "He's gone. I told him not to leave. He wouldn't have left without calling me first."

"Maybe the officer sent to check on Jose has him." Carter dialed the duty officer to see who was sent to check on Jose. Carter was connected with the officer.

Rosa could tell by Carter's expression the news wasn't good.

Carter ended the call. "He said when he arrived no one answered the door, so he had the hotel manager open the door for him and the room was empty."

Nine

Jose woke to the sound of someone pounding on the door. He opened the door half asleep, thinking Maria had returned and forgotten her key. But instead, an officer was standing in front of him.

"Are you Jose? Detective Carter sent me to pick you up and bring you to him."

"My Aunt Maria told me not to leave the room."

"Your Aunt Maria is with Detective Carter and will meet you at the station."

Jose decided it was safe to go with the police officer. He followed him to his patrol car leaving via the side door off the laundry room.

Excited to be riding in a police cruiser he asked, "Can I sit in the front with you and turn on the sirens?"

"No, civilians aren't allowed to ride up front," The officer gruffly replied as he opened the back door for Jose.

Jose slid inside and immediately felt on edge at the sight of the cage between him and the officer. He asked questions to hide his nervousness. "Have you ever shot anyone?"

"Not today," the officer laughed.

Jose didn't think it was very funny. "How much further before we get to the station?"

"I need to make a stop on the way first."

The officer parked in a handicap parking space close to a building. Jose looked up at the high rise in front of him.

"Come inside with me. It'll only take a minute."

Jose stepped out of the patrol car. He glanced up at the very tall building before following the officer inside. They entered the elevator and Jose watched as the officer pressed the button for the fifteenth floor. They rode all the way to top. When the door opened they were in an enormous room decorated with fancy furniture, artwork, and vases. The officer suddenly became nervous.

"Here is the delivery the boss requested," he said as he reached for Jose's arm.

Before Jose realized what was happening, he was shoved into the grips of a huge man. He was pulled into a room with a large desk. An older, very tan man was sitting behind the desk.

"Well, well, who do we have here?"

"This is the boy you asked for, sir."

"Boy, what's your name?"

"Jose," he said softly.

"Are Teo and Marcus your uncles?"

"Yeah."

The man picked up the phone and waited for someone to answer. Jose listened intently in disbelief. "I have your nephew. If you want him returned alive, you'll deliver me my money."

✲✲✲

Carter couldn't believe he had lost Jose once again. He tried not to panic and took control. "He couldn't have gotten too far. Maria, why don't you check the pool area to make sure he didn't go for a swim. Rosa and I will review the camera footage from the lobby. If Jose left unwillingly maybe we can see who took him."

Carter approached the front desk and asked for the hotel manager. He explained the situation and their urgent need to review any video footage. The manager took Rosa and Carter to an office. The manager fast forwarded through the video from that morning.

"There, stop the video!"

The manager pressed pause to freeze the picture.

"That's not the officer that was assigned to pick up Jose," Carter explained. "Keep playing and let's see if he returns."

They watched the rest of the video but the officer never returned and there was no footage of Jose leaving the building.

"Do you have any other video cameras that might show where the officer went after he left the lobby?" Carter asked.

"Yes. We also have cameras located on the side exits that I can show you."

"Great! Can we watch the video footage from them this morning?"

The manager brought up the video from the other cameras and fast forwarded until Rosa yelled, "Stop!"

The frame froze, showing Jose following the police officer they saw entering the lobby. "Okay, continue playing the video slowly forward," Carter said. He stared at the screen, trying to find any clues as to where Jose was going and who the officer was that took him. He watched as Jose exited the hotel with the police officer.

Rosa spoke up. "I have a bad feeling about this. I thought it was strange every time we got close to catching up with Jose he disappeared again."

"What do you mean?" Carter asked.

"You take Jose to your place. In the middle of the night someone kidnaps him. There was only one other person that even knew Jose was staying with you. Then you get a call from Father Benito to let you know he has Jose. But before you arrive, Diego shows up. Now, you tell a duty officer where Jose is located and he disappears again. Too many incidents to be a coincidence and this footage proves it. We have a rat within our own police department."

"That, unfortunately, is my suspicion also, but I didn't want to believe it. Can you make us a copy of the video?" Carter asked the manager.

"Sure, no problem. Just give me a second to find a spare disc to use."

With a copy of the video in hand, Carter and Rosa found Maria waiting for them in the lobby.

"I can't find Jose anywhere. Did you have any luck?"

Carter shared with her what they saw on the video.

Maria had an idea and relayed it to them. "Since Marcus isn't in the morgue, he must be alive somewhere. Let me try his cell phone one more time and see if I can get him to answer."

Carter felt like an idiot for forgetting about Marcus not being dead. He could play a key role in finding who took Jose. "Can you put it on speaker so we can listen?"

"Yes." Maria dialed the number and they waited as the phone rang. She prayed he would answer.

"Hello."

"Marcus, is that you?" Maria asked.

"Yes."

"Are you all right?"

"I don't have time to explain everything to you right now. I'll get back with you later today."

"Where are you?"

"It is best I don't give you that information yet. I don't want to put you in harms way."

"Is Jose with you?"

"No, but I know where he is and who has him. I'll call you back as soon as I can."

"I'm here with Detective Carter. Tell him what's going on so he can help."

"I can't involve the police or they'll kill Jose. Don't worry, I'll fix this. I have to go."

Before Maria could say another word the phone call ended.

"Maria, I think it would be safer for you to stay in your hotel room with the door locked until we figure out what's going on," Carter said. "Here's my cell number in case you hear from Marcus or Jose. Will you give me Marcus' cell phone number so we can try to track it?"

"Of course." Carter handed Maria his cell phone. She entered Marcus' phone number.

Rosa could see the concern on Maria's face. "Try not to worry. With any luck we can get Marcus to lead us to where Jose is being held. If we can't track Marcus' cell, we should be able to identity the officer who took Jose. As soon as we locate the officer we will make him tell us where Jose is."

They turned to leave when Carter remembered one more thing, "Don't talk to any other officers until we know who we can trust. I'll give you a call as soon as we track down Jose and Marcus."

Time was of the essence. Carter had a bad feeling Jose's luck was running out. They needed to hurry.

Ten

Marcus knew what he had to do. He retrieved the million dollars that Teo had placed in the trunk of his car and drove to the address given to him by the caller. He had to somehow figure out how to exchange the money for Jose without getting them both killed. The caller had told him to arrive at 3PM. He looked nervously at his watch. It was two thirty. He forced himself to drive the speed limit. The last thing he needed was to be pulled over by the police for speeding. How would he explain the million dollars he had in his back seat? He was still ten miles away and hoped that traffic wouldn't cause him to be late. He exited highway 95 and made his way toward the beach. He parked in front of the address given to him, a new condominium complex located on the beach. He glanced at his watch. It was now two fifty-five. He needed to hurry. He grabbed the suitcase from the back seat and cautiously entered the building. He was greeted by two large men that escorted him to the elevator.

Marcus rode the elevator in silence with the two men by his side. When the elevator door opened, the men each grabbed one of his arms. They forcefully took the suitcase full of money from his grasp, then shoved him into a room. His eyes were drawn to a gray haired man, dressed in a nice suit, sitting behind an executive style Mahoney desk. The view behind the desk was breathtaking. Crystal blue water flowed over the edgeless pool on the patio. This allowed an unobstructed view of the glittering ocean swells spread out as far as the eye could see.

The man behind the desk spoke, "Did you bring me my money?"

"Yes, Teo tried to deliver it to you but was ambushed at the marina. Now that I have done as you asked, can I have my nephew?"

94

"It's not that simple. You see, your brother and I had an arrangement. He made sure my drugs were safely delivered into this country. In exchange I made him a very wealthy man and promised not hurt his family."

"My brother honored his part in the arrangement, that is until he was killed."

"Your brother's sloppy work has brought the police snooping around my business. I need some assurance that you won't lead them to me." An evil smile came to his face.

"You can trust me. All I want to do is leave with my nephew and return to Belize. I have no desire to stay in Miami any longer then necessary or ever return."

"Bring Jose here," he instructed one of his men.

Marcus eagerly watched for Jose to appear. The side door opened and Jose stared up at him.

"Jose, are you hurt?" Marcus asked. He kneeled down to the boy's level to check him over.

Jose touched his face. "Aunt Maria told me you were dead."

"She was mistaken." Marcus held Jose's hand and they started toward the door.

"Where do you think you're going?"

"You have your money and I have Jose. Our business is complete."

The man laughed. "You don't think I'm just going to let you walk out of here? You know too much."

Marcus suddenly realized he wasn't going to let them live. The man nodded to his men. The unspoken command was understood by them. Marcus was firmly grabbed by the arms and led toward the elevator. Another man reached for Jose. Marcus wasn't going to die without a fight. He had to save Jose. The men stopped at the elevator. Marcus heard the ding indicating the elevator had arrived and the door was about to open. He started punching and kicking with all his might. He yelled, "Run Jose!"

Then gunfire erupted. Marcus found himself on the floor, unable to determine if Jose had reached the elevator unharmed.

***

Carter and Rosa got a break. Marcus' cell phone was off so they weren't able to trace it but they identified the officer that had taken Jose. His name was Stanley Chester. He was employed as a police officer at the south side precinct. Carter didn't hesitate after receiving this information. He immediately headed to his Mustang with Rosa following close behind. He raced through town with his blue lights flashing through his front grill and siren blaring to alert the other drivers to get out of his way. As Carter approached the south side police department he turned off his siren and lights. He needed the element of surprise to not alert Stanley Chester he was coming. He didn't know who he could trust and needed to find a way to locate the officer without generating any suspicion. He slowly drove through the parking area, looking for the patrol car number spotted on the hotel surveillance video.

Rosa spotted the cruiser in the parking lot first. "There it is! He must be somewhere inside. If this guy is as big of a jerk as I think he is, I can play on his ego. I'll go inside and identify myself as a detective. I'll make it known that I need Officer Stanley Chester's assistance with a case I'm working. When I find Stanley I'll explain I have a case that needs his special attention, that only he can help me with. I'll give him my helpless female officer routine, if you know what I mean. Then I'll ask him to follow me to my car so I can show him the evidence we confiscated for his evaluation." Maria winked at Carter.

"Are you sure? There is no telling how many officers are in on this. If someone identifies you and figures out what you're up to, this might not go as planned."

"I can take care of myself. Do you have a better idea?"

Carter had to admit, Rosa did have a way of persuading men to do as she asked. "All right, I don't like it but right now that seems like our best bet. If you don't come back out in fifteen minutes I'm coming in looking for you. Agreed?"

96

"Agreed. But trust me, no one can resist this," she said as she motioned to her sexy body. She was wearing tight black jeans with a white buttoned up blouse. She undid the top two buttons of her blouse to expose more of her cleavage. She untied her ponytail, fluffed her black, curly hair, then applied red lipstick to her voluptuous lips. "I'll be right back." Rosa smiled and winked at Carter as she left, swaying her nicely rounded behind as she walked away.

Carter forced himself to take his eyes off Rosa and slouched down in his seat so he wouldn't be seen.

Rosa approached the front desk and gave the officer manning the desk one of her big Puerto Rican smiles. "I need to speak with Stanley Chester."

After some flirtatious comments, he was very accommodating. "You should be able to find Stanley in the break room."

Rosa found the break area and entered. She immediately recognized Stanley from his face on the hotel video footage. He was talking with several officers. They stopped talking when they saw her approach.

"Hi, officers," Rosa said as she pushed her hair over her shoulder. "I was hoping to get a minute of Officer Chester's time."

Stanley Chester spoke up. "You seem to know me but I don't recall ever meeting you?"

Rosa introduced herself as a detective from the north precinct. She explained her desperate need for his assistance with a case. After some razing from the other officers, he agreed to follow her to the car where she needed to show him something she found at the crime scene. Rosa could tell his interest was peaked. As predicted, he was more than happy to follow her to the Mustang. She opened the passenger door.

Officer Chester looked inside and suddenly there was a gun pointed at his face. "Hey, what is this?"

Rosa stuck her gun into his back, "Get in the back seat and don't make any sudden moves or I might have to shoot you."

Carter smiled at Rosa as she slid into the back seat with Stanley, securely restraining him in handcuffs. She removed his gun from his holster. "You won't be needing this." She handed the gun to Carter.

"We're going to take you for a little ride and if you answer our questions, then we might not kill you before we arrest you. Do you understand?" Rosa said letting him see her not so nice girly side. She made it perfectly clear she wouldn't hesitate to shoot him if he tried anything.

"What is this about?"

"Don't play games with us, Stanley. I think you know what this is about. First, we know you took Jose from his hotel room this morning. So don't even try to deny it. All we want to know is where you took him."

"I'm a dead man if I give you that information so you might as well go ahead and kill me now."

Rosa's elbow suddenly made contact with Officer Chester's nose. "Oops, my arm must have slipped."

"You broke my nose, bitch!" He reached for his face as blood gushed out of his nose.

"Next it's your knee unless you start talking."

"You'll never get away with this."

"Oh really? I'm sure the FBI will love to hear about how a police officer assisted in the kidnapping of a child, sex trafficking, and distribution of drugs. I'm sure they'll find a real safe place for you in Federal Prison."

"If I tell you what you want to know, how are you going to protect me?"

"You tell us where Jose is located and who instructed you to take him, we let you go and you disappear. We'll not report you to the FBI or file any charges against you. That is the deal. Take it or leave it."

"So I tell you where I dropped off Jose, who asked me to, and you are just going to let me walk away?"

"Yes, once we confirm Jose is where you say he is. It'll be up to you to save your own ass and get out of town before they find you," Carter added.

"Start talking," Rosa stuck her gun firmly into his ribs.

"I was told to deliver him to the Ocean View condominium complex. The request came from the captain at your precinct."

Carter was not expecting that. "Are you telling me the captain is working for J. R. Dragone?"

"Yes, I told you what you wanted to know, now let me go."

Carter made a u-turn and turned on his siren and lights as he weaved through traffic. He raced to the Ocean View condominium complex. He stopped about a block away and parked. "What floor did you deliver him to?"

"I took him to the fifteenth floor where Dragone's office is located. You'll never be able to get in there. He has armed guards standing by the elevator at all times."

"Cuff him to the arm rest so he doesn't get away while we confirm Jose is inside," Carter winked at Rosa.

Rosa understood the wink and loosely cuffed Officer Chester's wrist to the arm rest.

Carter and Rosa exited the car and cautiously walked toward the condominium complex.

"I assume you have a plan?" Rosa asked.

"Yeah. My plan is we'll figure it out as we go."

"Really, that's your plan?"

They approached the entrance to the building. Carter pulled his baseball cap over his eyes to conceal his face from any security cameras. "I'll go in first to make sure the entrance to the elevator is clear. Then you follow and we can ride the elevator up together. I know this could be dangerous and a little crazy. I'll understand if you want to wait here for me to return," Carter said.

"No way I'm letting you have all the fun," Rosa smiled.

Carter slipped inside the building and it was eerily quiet. There wasn't anyone in the lobby and Carter wasn't sure that was a good sign. He pushed the up button for the elevator and the door immediately opened. He glanced back at the entrance and Rosa rushed toward him. They slipped into the plush elevator together before they were seen. Knowing there was probably a camera in the elevator that would announce their arrival, they waited until the last minute to draw their weapons. They didn't know what would be waiting for them on the other side of the elevator door. Carter counted the dings as the elevator raced toward the fifteenth floor. The elevator door started to open and Carter yelled, "Now!" They both drew their guns, ready for the battle that awaited them.

Carter was surprised at what he saw. There was already a fight in progress as the door opened. Jose's frightened face appeared, standing right in front of him. Rosa started shooting as the men throwing punches drew their weapons. Carter forcefully pulled Jose into the elevator. He pushed the first floor button, stepping through the elevator door before it closed. He wanted Jose away from the danger. Then he joined the fight as more men came running toward them with guns drawn, firing. Rosa and Carter worked in harmony, each hitting their target and moving around the room until there were no more men standing. Eight men lay bleeding on the floor. Carter cleared the remaining rooms while Rosa made sure the injured men didn't get up.

"All clear! Dragone must have slipped out the emergency exit," Carter said.

One of the guys sat up on the floor and raised his hands above his head. "My name is Marcus. I'm Jose's uncle. I was just trying to rescue him."

"So you're Marcus? I don't know what you and your brother got yourself into, but we need to get you out of here before the police arrive. Rosa, take Marcus down to the lobby and find Jose. Don't let anyone see you. I'll make sure no one here does anything stupid."

Marcus was shocked by the officers response, but didn't argue. He stepped into the elevator and that's when he saw the blood.

Rosa followed Marcus into the elevator. She pushed the button for the lobby. "Well, Marcus, you have a lot of explaining to do." Then Rosa noticed what Marcus was looking at. "Are you bleeding?"

"No, that isn't my blood."

The elevator door finally opened. They rushed to find Jose. His limp body lay on the floor not far from the elevator.

Carter used his cell phone to call for backup and an ambulance. Then he called Rosa to make sure she had Jose. "Do you have Jose? Is he okay?"

There was a pause and at first Carter thought the call had dropped. "Rosa, is he with you?"

"Yes, he's been shot. I'm trying to stop the bleeding but it's bad. Marcus is going to take us to the hospital in his brother's car."

"I'll catch up with you once I explain this mess to the arriving officers. Keep Marcus out of sight," Carter said.

"What about Officer Chester?"

"I'm sure by now he's found a way to get out of the handcuffs and is miles away, trying to disappear before Dragone finds out he was the rat."

They hung up and Carter waited for reinforcements to arrive. He knew he was going to have a lot of explaining to do.

Several hours passed and the scene was finally cleared. Carter explained several times that he had received an anonymous tip that Jose was being held on the fifteenth floor of the condominium complex and that he had no idea that the unit belonged to J. R. Dragone. That he and Rosa were ransacked as soon as the elevator door opened and they had no choice but to shoot all eight gunmen to save their own lives. He continued to explain that Jose was injured in the process and, due to his life threatening injuries, Rosa had immediately taken him to the hospital. There was no mention of Marcus or Officer Chester being involved in the explanation. After several hours of questioning, Carter returned to his Mustang. He found the handcuffs that had once secured Officer Chester still hanging from the arm rest without the officer inside them. He used a rag and some water he had in the truck to clean Officer Chester's blood from his nice leather seat. He drove to the precinct after being summoned by a very angry captain.

Carter walked directly to the captain's office, knowing he was going to be reprimanded for what had just happened.

"You better have a good explanation for your behavior this afternoon," the captain said.

Carter knew he had to tread lightly, knowing the captain was the one leaking Jose's whereabouts to Dragone. "Sir, I received an anonymous tip letting me know where Jose was being held. I didn't have time to coordinate back up for fear Jose may have been hurt."

"That is the best excuse you could come up with? You didn't have thirty seconds to call me and make me aware of the situation before you ransacked the condominium, causing many casualties and disturbing many prominent residents of this community?" the Captain asked as his face turned beet red. "And your hostage was injured in the process! The only explanation you can give me is you didn't have time!"

"With the delicate nature of this case, I hoped I could extract Jose from his kidnappers without causing additional bloodshed. I'm very sorry sir, for the outcome."

"I'm removing you and your partner from this case. Now that you've found Jose the investigation can be closed."

Carter knew he would only dig a deeper hole for himself if he tried to argue with the captain. He turned to leave the captain's office, then immediately left the precinct, got in his car and called Rosa on his way to the hospital. "How is Jose?"

"He's still in surgery."

Carter could hear the sadness and fatigue in her voice. "You know me, I'm not a religious person, but I've been praying that God will let this poor kid live. He didn't deserve this," Carter said. "Did you find a safe place for Marcus?"

"Yes. After I dropped Jose off at the emergency room I took Marcus to the hotel where Maria was staying. I called Maria on the way to let her know I was coming and what car I would be in. I told her to check out and meet me in the lobby. You should've seen her face when she got in the car and saw Marcus in the back seat! I've never seen two people so happy to see each other. I took them to my apartment until we could come up with something better. I backed Teo's car into a parking space so no one could see the license plate, and took my car back to the hospital. That being said, how am I going to explain that I'm harboring a murderer?"

"I'm about five minutes away from the hospital and I'll catch you up when I arrive."

***

Carter found Rosa in the emergency room waiting area sipping a cup of coffee. He shared with her his version of the events leading up to Jose being shot that he had told the other officers and the captain. "Oh, I saved the worst for last. We have both been removed from the case."

"Well, this is a good mess you've gotten us into," Rosa said.

"I know and I'm going to fix it. Since we don't know who we can trust within our own department I contacted a friend of mine that works for the FBI. I explained our situation and the importance of keeping Marcus safely hidden and protecting Jose. I plan to put Maria, Jose, and Marcus in protective custody once I hear Marcus' side of the story. He obviously can connect Dragone to Jose's kidnapping and probably more. I'm sure Dragone will go out of his way to find Marcus and make sure he can't talk. Right now no one other than my friend in the FBI knows we have Marcus. I told him I would contact him and set up a safe place to hand him over shortly."

"What about Jose? We need to contact his mother and let her know that Jose has been injured. I told Maria as soon as he's out of surgery I would let her know so she could contact her sister to explain everything."

"I'll arrange to have Jose's mother flown to Miami so she can stay with him during his recovery," Carter said.

"You're assuming he'll survive," Rosa said.

"Right now I can't imagine any other possible outcome. If he dies I'll never be able to forgive myself."

"It's not your fault he got shot."

"I know, but if I had stopped him from being abducted from my apartment in the first place, he wouldn't be in the shape he's in now."

A doctor approached and Carter and Rosa stood up from their seats. "Jose made it through surgery. We managed to stop the internal bleeding. Now it's up to him. He'll stay in ICU until we are sure the bleeding is under control and he's not at risk for an infection. The next twenty four hours are critical. I'm going to keep him sedated to reduce his pain level so he can heal."

"Thank you doctor." Carter breathed a sigh of relief.

"Now that we know Jose is in good hands, why don't you go to my place and update Maria and Marcus on Jose's status? Then talk to Marcus and find out what happened and how much he knows. I'll stand guard here tonight to make sure no one tries to harm Jose further," Rosa said.

"I'll call you later to fill you in on Marcus' explanation of events. Once I hear back from my FBI friend, I'll let you know how we plan to bring down Dragone and the captain. I'll arrange to have someone I trust relieve you so you can get some rest. I don't have to tell you, but if Jose wakes up, don't let any police officers speak to him. We still don't know which officers are on Dragone's payroll that might want to harm Jose," Carter said.

"The doctor will limit access to him as long as he's in ICU. That should give us some time," Rosa added.

"Thanks for covering my back today. I promise you I'll find a way to get us out of this mess," Carter said as he left.

✳✳✳

Carter arrived at Rosa's apartment with a large pepperoni pizza in hand. He removed Rosa's spare key from above the door jamb and let himself in. He announced his arrival so he wouldn't scare Marcus and Maria. "It's Carter! Is anyone hungry for Chinese food?"

Maria and Marcus emerged from the bedroom. "Thank goodness it's you! When we heard the door being opened we hid in the closet just in case Dragone figured out where we were staying. How is Jose?" Marcus asked.

"He's out of surgery and being monitored overnight to make sure he doesn't start bleeding again. From what I've seen, he is a very strong kid. I have faith he'll make a full recovery."

"Thanks for bringing us a bit of good news," Maria said. "I need to call Sophia and let her know."

"Before you call, let me reserve her an airline ticket for tomorrow. I know she is desperate to see him."

"She'll be thrilled to finally be reunited with Jose and see how he's doing for herself."

Carter managed to purchase her a seat on a flight arriving at 9AM the next morning. He told Maria, "Tell Sophia we will meet her just past the airport security checkpoint. Then I'll take us to the hospital."

Maria called Sophia and shared the good news with her. "Pack your bags and make sure you are on the early morning flight to Miami!"

While Maria finished discussing Jose's status and travel arrangements with Sophia, Carter found some plates and glasses in the kitchen. As soon as Maria ended the call Carter spoke up, "Now that that is settled, let's eat some food before it gets cold." Carter handed them each a plate and a glass of soda.

While they ate Carter decided it was as good as time as any to see what Marcus would share with him. "Marcus, Jose told me he saw you kill a man in the cargo area of the Belize airplane. He

105

also shared with me that you were in the vehicle when sister Angelia was shot. I would like to hear your side of the story."

Marcus was surprised by Carter's accusations. "I'd never kill anyone and don't even own a gun."

"So start from the beginning and tell me how you ended up helping your brother."

"My brother, Teo, called me out of the blue last week after I hadn't heard from him in almost five years. He said he had been traveling between Belize and Miami, working for a man transporting some goods for him. He said he needed my help to watch his back for one last job, then he would have enough money to return to Belize for good. He said he had met someone. He was ready to settle down and get married. I only agreed to help him because I thought if I did this favor for him, he would finally come home and be apart of our family again. I knew Maria wouldn't approve of me helping my brother, so I told her I had some business to take care of and would be back in a couple of days. I flew to Miami, as instructed by Teo, and picked up a duffle bag with red tape on the handle. I caught a taxi and gave the driver the address to Teo's apartment. That's where Teo had told me to meet him. As the taxi pulled away from the transportation area at the airport, I looked out the window, and couldn't believe my eyes. I saw Jose getting on a tour bus. By the time the taxi was able to stop and go back to the baggage area, the tour bus had disappeared. About that time my cell phone rang and it was Maria letting me know Jose was missing."

Carter stopped him from continuing. "So since you say you didn't kill the man in the cargo area of the airplane, could Jose have seen Teo kill the man instead of you? You are brothers and look a lot alike."

"It's possible. Teo said he was traveling between Belize and Miami so he may have been in Belize when he contacted me."

"That might explain why Jose said he saw you kill the man. Jose was hiding in the cargo area of the airplane at the time of the killing."

Maria spoke up, "That poor child! How terrified he must've been!"

"Continue with your story. You were heading to the address of the apartment when you spotted Jose get on the tour bus."

"I explained to Maria on the phone that I would find Jose and not to worry. The taxi took me to the address Teo had provided. Teo told me to wait at the apartment for him to arrive. While I waited I found the number of the tour bus that I saw Jose get on. That's when I discovered the tour bus was going to a Disney World Resort Hotel outside Orlando. I had no way to drive to the hotel so I had to wait until Teo arrived that evening. When Teo finally arrived his only interest was in making sure the duffle bag I picked up from the airport had all of its contents. He was furious when he found out there were a few bags missing. Teo made some phone calls and told me a boy had taken some of his merchandise. He showed me a blurry image of the boy sent to his iPhone. I couldn't believe my eyes! It was Jose! Teo had last seen Jose when he was only five years old so he didn't recognize him. I explained to Teo about the tour bus and where it had taken Jose. So we left late that night for the Disney World Resort to find Jose. We arrived just after sunrise. The only clue I had to Jose's whereabouts was the shuttle bus destination. When we arrived at the hotel and walked into the lobby, something caught my eye darting out the side door. It was Jose. I tried to catch up with him but he was too fast. He ran through some high bushes and between some buildings and I lost him. Teo and I returned to his SUV and drove around all day trying to find him. We were just about to give up when we drove by a park. I spotted Jose with a lady. Teo didn't want me approaching Jose with the woman next to him, so we followed her to a house and watched Jose go inside. Teo was very paranoid and thought it might be a trap. So we waited, parked just down the road, until all the lights went out in the house. Then Teo wanted me to sneak into the house, quietly pick up Jose, and hopefully the rest of his merchandise. I wasn't thrilled with this idea but agreed to go along with Teo so Jose wouldn't get hurt. Before I could break in though, Jose walked out the back of the house and started down the street. Teo drove up beside him and I grabbed him. After he saw that it was me, he stopped fighting. Teo asked him about the jelly beans he had stolen from the airplane. Jose told us that he had left them in the house. Teo turned around and went back to the house. He told Jose to go back inside, retrieve the jelly beans, and come right back. But instead of Jose coming out by himself with the jelly beans, the lady we had seen him with earlier approached our vehicle with the bags of jelly beans in her hand. Teo freaked. After she handed me the bags of jelly beans, he shot her, and sped off without Jose. By the time I got Teo to calm down and turn around to pick up Jose, the place was swarming with police."

"So you just left your nephew at a strangers house where the owner had just been shot?" Maria asked angrily.

"I know how it sounds. I should've made Teo turn around and let me out of the car. He convinced me, though that Jose was in good hands with the police. That they would take good care of him and return him to his mother. Teo said he was running out of time and needed to return to Miami to make the exchange before it was too late. By the time we arrived back at the apartment in Miami the sun was coming up. Teo took the bags of jelly beans we retrieved from Jose and opened them to make sure the product was all there. That's when he realized he had been tricked. He had received real jelly beans instead of the merchandise he was expecting. He said it was too late to return to Orlando, that the drop was scheduled for midnight. He hid the fake merchandise at the bottom of the duffle bag and hoped it wouldn't be discovered until he was long gone. The rest of the afternoon I tried to get some rest but I was too worried about Jose and the upcoming exchange. I imagined everything that could possible go wrong. I wanted to call Maria and let her know where Jose was but knew she wouldn't be happy with my explanation. I thought if I waited until this mess with my brother was resolved she would understand why I did what I did. Teo was no longer the loving brother I remembered. I considered walking away and leaving Teo before the exchange. I being the big brother though, always felt it was my responsibility to protect Teo. But I wasn't sure I could protect him this time. I had to try, or I would blame myself if anything happened to him. I knew in my heart I had to see this thing through no matter how mad I was at him. So, a little before midnight, we drove to a remote swampy area west of Miami. The exchange went off without a hitch and Teo drove away with one and a half million dollars. Half a million was his. The remaining million was to be delivered to someone else."

"Did you see the faces or hear any names of the people he met at the exchange?"

"No, it was dark and I stayed in the car. I was just there in case Teo needed me to get him out of harm's way."

"So what happened to the million dollars he was to deliver?"

"I'm getting to that. After the exchange, we headed back to Teo's apartment. Before we arrived, Teo's cell phone rang. Whoever he talked to told him that Jose was back in Miami and gave him the address where he was staying. Teo said we could pick Jose up on the way back to his place."

"That must've been when the captain shared that I was keeping Jose at my place."

"That was your place where Teo stopped to get Jose?"

"Yes. What did Teo tell you?"

"Well we arrived, I guess at your apartment complex, and Teo told me to stay in the car. He said that Jose was expecting him and that he would be right back. I didn't know Teo planned on kidnapping him until I saw Teo running toward the car with Jose under his arm. Jose was still wearing pajamas. He threw Jose in the back, jumped in the drivers seat, and sped off. Teo's apartment was only a couple of blocks away so he hurriedly parked and directed me to take Jose upstairs. Jose was obviously upset and I tried to calm him down and let him know he was safe. I checked to make sure Jose wasn't injured and left him sitting on the sofa while I talked to Teo in the Kitchen. I asked Teo what the hell had he just done! That's when Teo explained that he was hoping to find the rest of the drugs but ran out of time when a crazy bird started making all kinds of noise."

Carter laughed, "Yes, that was my Macaw. He alerted me to an intruder. Continue."

"After talking with Teo I discovered he had kidnapped Jose from a police officer's home, instead of having permission like he told me. I was furious with Teo and told him I was done. I was leaving with Jose as soon as the sun came up. Teo begged me to stay. He said he needed me one last time. He still had to turn over the million dollars at the marina at 7AM. He wanted me to watch his back one last time and make sure he wasn't being set up. It was already 5AM and I agreed to this one last favor. I just wanted to get it over with and go home. Since it was still the middle of the night, I returned to the living room and showed Jose to the bedroom. I locked Jose inside before we left so I didn't have to worry about him running away. I left Jose asleep. Teo gave me the keys to a separate car and instructed me to follow him to the marina."

"So Teo drove his SUV and what car did you drive?"

"It was a maroon four door Nissan Altima that Rosa drove us here in. Teo placed the million dollars in the trunk of my car. He told me that once he had determined it wasn't a trap, he would motion for me to join him on the dock with the bag of money. I parked in the marina parking area away from his car and watched for his signal for me to come with the money. I noticed two fishermen walking down the dock and before I realized what was happening, I heard multiple gunshots. Once the gunfire erupted, two more people ran down the dock toward the yacht, with weapons drawn. I feared the worse and decided it was best for me to leave."

"Those other two people were Rosa and I. We were given a tip about a possible drug exchange and that Jose might have been at the Marina. The two fisherman were drug enforcement officers.

110

During the exchange of gunfire Teo was shot and killed instantly. There was nothing I could do for him."

"I don't blame you. I know Teo brought this on himself. I was fooling myself to think I could bring him back home and have it be like it used to be when we were kids."

"So did Teo say anything about a human trafficking operation?"

"Teo told me he transported merchandise and didn't get into the details. What did you find on the boat?"

"There were several young women that had been tied up and drugged."

"Where were they taken from?"

"They were all from Mexico."

"I'm sorry Teo didn't share anything with me about any girls being on the boat. It's hard for me to believe that Teo would've had anything to do with human trafficking. But obviously I didn't know what my brother was capable of."

"Where did you go after the Marina?"

"I was worried for Jose's safety and didn't want to return to Teo's apartment with a trunk full of money. I called my friend Diego. I asked him to pick up Jose and take him someplace safe. He said he would take him to his sister's house."

"So Diego was telling us the truth," Carter added.

"You talked to Diego?"

"Yes, I thought he had kidnapped Jose, but it was just a misunderstanding. Continue. What happened next?"

"I told Diego I would pick up Jose in a few hours. I hadn't slept in two days and needed time to rest and think. I drove north on 95 until I felt I was a safe distance away from Miami and that no one was following me. I exited at West Palm Beach and drove to the coast. I checked into a hotel using a fake name and paid cash. I was exhausted. I entered the room, collapsed on the bed, and turned on the television. The news was on. The anchor reported two men were killed by police at a marina. I still had a bit of hope that Teo wasn't one of those men. I thought he might be in a jail cell and wouldn't be able to contact me until he was released.

After several hours I still hadn't heard from Teo and feared the worst. I remembered the Teo I grew up with that was full of life and ideas. He didn't want to work in the fields any longer. As soon as he was old enough, he left one night and disappeared. I had hoped his dreams had come true. I never would have imagined Teo doing anything illegal to make a living. We weren't raised that way."

"After you got to the hotel what happened?"

"Diego called to let me know Jose was safe at his sister's. I told him I needed a little more time and asked if I could pick Jose up the next day. He said that wouldn't be a problem. After passing out from exhaustion and sleeping through the night, I came up with a plan. I decided to stash the money in the spare tire wheel well in case I was stopped by the police. Then I would return to Miami to be reunited with Jose and go home. The only problem was, when I arrived at Diego's sister's house the next morning, Jose was gone. Juanita, Diego's sister, was furious at me. She told me Diego had been arrested for kidnapping and that it was all my fault. I was afraid to go to the police. Teo had told me a cop was the one that told him where Jose was being held. So I couldn't trust the police. I wandered the streets looking for Jose, with no luck, and spent another night in a hotel. I tried to reach Maria to see if she had heard from Jose, but didn't get an answer. I now know that was because she was on her way to Miami to identify a body she thought to be me." Marcus looked at Maria with a defeated sad face. "I can't imagine what you must've gone through thinking I was dead, having to go to the morgue to identify my body, then discovering it wasn't me. I understand why you're mad at me. I have a lot to make up for." Marcus reached for Maria's hand.

Maria squeezed Marcus' hand. "I don't know if I should be furious with you or just be ecstatic that you are still alive!"

Marcus leaned over and kissed Maria on the lips to help take away her anger.

"So how did you end up in Dragone's condo?"

"While I was trying to figure out what to do next, my cell phone rang. I was hoping it was Maria saying Jose had been found. But it was a guy instead, telling me he had Jose and if I wanted to see him alive, to deliver the money to him immediately. He gave me an address. I removed the money from the spare tire compartment, then drove to the address provided. I was met at the elevator, frisked for weapons, then taken to the fifteenth floor where I was introduced to Mr. Dragone. I made the exchange and asked him to hand over Jose as promised. He had other plans though. He was going to have us both killed. I decided I wasn't going to go out without a fight. I thought I could at least save Jose. So just before the elevator door opened, and you arrived, I started fighting with all my might. I told Jose to get in the elevator and run. That's when you showed up and all hell broke loose."

"I'm sure you've figured out by now that you're in the middle of something very dangerous. Dragone managed to escape before we could capture him at his condo. I know he won't hesitate to kill you to prevent you from talking. I contacted a friend with the FBI that I would trust with my life. He's willing to take you into protective custody until Dragone can be put behind bars."

"I don't want to spend the rest of my life looking over my shoulder, worrying about my family being hurt. What do we need to do to put Dragone away for life so I can return to Belize and sleep peacefully?"

"I might have a plan, but it will be dangerous for you."

"After what I've been through I'm sure I can handle it. Just tell me what I need to do to get this bastard."

"First we need to get Maria, Jose, and Sophia someplace safe so they don't become targets or pawns. It involves me arresting you so the dirty cops can contact Dragone to tell him your whereabouts."

"Are you still in?"

"Yes." Marcus held out his wrists to be cuffed.

"It's been a very long day. It's almost midnight and we all need some rest before we start my scheme. You two sleep in Rosa's bed and I'll sleep on the sofa. I'll contact my friend with the FBI in the morning and start everything in motion."

***

Carter woke early, still in the same clothes he had worn the previous day. He quietly dialed Rosa's cell phone, not wanting to wake up Marcus and Maria.

"How are you holding up, and how is Jose?"

"I'm fighting to stay awake and Jose did well overnight. His vital signs are strong and there is no sign of bleeding. It was quiet with no unexpected visitors."

"Good. An FBI agent should arrive any minute to relieve you. I plan to pick up Sophia, Jose's mother, at the airport at nine o'clock. I'll transport her to the hospital. Then I plan to arrest Marcus." Carter proceeded to bring Rosa up to speed on Marcus' account of events over the last week and the fact that he didn't kill the man in the cargo area of the airplane. He also explained to Rosa how he was going to catch Dragone and the police officers involved.

"You know your plan is just crazy enough to work," Rosa said.

"Thanks for your vote of confidence," Carter joked. "Get some rest and hopefully, if all goes as planned, I'll see you soon."

Carter contacted Alex, his FBI friend next. He quickly brought him up to speed. Alex agreed to set up the necessary resources to ensure Carter's plan worked.

Now that everything was set in place, Carter searched for coffee and something to eat for breakfast. Rosa's kitchen cabinets were just about as bare as his, a sign that they both worked too many hours. He found a large can of coffee. He dumped six heaping spoonfuls of grounds into the filter and filled the coffee maker with water. The strong brew was just what he needed to stay alert. He couldn't take any chance of making a mistake today or Marcus may lose his life. Next he found a box of cereal and a gallon of milk in the refrigerator. He smelled the milk and was pleasantly surprised that it wasn't sour. The aroma of coffee woke Maria and Marcus. They joined Carter in the kitchen.

"Good morning. I hope you were able to put today out of your mind and get a little rest?" Carter asked.

"Not much. I'm ready to get this day over with," Marcus said.

"I understand. Have a bowl of cereal and a cup coffee. While you eat, I'll explain what I'm going to need from you today." They both sat at the kitchen table with Carter and listened intently as he outlined his plan. They sipped their coffee and tried to stomach a little food as Carter went over the details.

"Maria, I want you to go to the airport with me to pick up your sister. You'll be safe with her at the hospital. An FBI agent will be standing guard outside Jose's room. Marcus, after I drop them off at the hospital I'll come back here to arrest you and take you in for questioning. I'll need you to recount your story about Dragone being the one responsible for the drug smuggling and kidnapping of Jose. Also, how you managed to get away when Rosa and I started shooting."

"Understood. I'll say I saw Dragone head for the back exit. I followed him to escape capture and to get away from the flying bullets. Once outside I drove to a rest area and slept in the backseat of my car until I figured out what to do next. In the morning I turned on my cell phone and called Maria. She persuaded me I needed to turn myself into you."

"Very good, that sounds believable. After I take your statement I'll tell the captain I'm issuing a warrant for your arrest and taking you into protective custody so you can testify against Dragone. This'll be the bait I need to catch the captain relaying the information to Dragone. I have arranged for an FBI escort to take you to a safe house. But this will also be a decoy. To protect you from being killed by Dragone, I'm going to do a bait and switch as soon as we leave the station. When you make the first turn there will be a parking garage on your right. A van will be parked at the entrance. I need for you to jump out of the FBI vehicle and run into the parking garage before any of Dragone's men can see you. I'll

115

be waiting for you inside a dark green van with no passenger windows. Then I'll drive us to an undisclosed location that only me and my FBI friend know about. I'll provide you and Maria with a burner phone. That way you'll be able to communicate with her without being traced by anyone. Don't turn on your personal cell phone or attempt to use it or Dragone will be able to track your location. Understand?"

"Yes," Marcus held up his phone to show Carter it was off. "What will happen to Sophia, Jose, and Maria?"

"If everything goes as planned Dragone is going to think he killed you and that he's in the clear. We'll need to keep you out of sight until the trial is over."

"How long will that take?"

"I'll press the prosecutor for an expedient trial. Dragone is going to think we don't have any evidence against him with you supposedly dead. He'll want to put this behind him as soon as possible so he can resume business as usual. I know this is a lot to absorb. Unfortunately, Maria and I need to leave for the airport to pick up Sophia. Trust me, I'll get you through this."

Maria grabbed Marcus' hand and squeezed it. She leaned over and kissed him on the lips. "I love you and I'll see you soon. Take care of yourself."

Carter hoped Maria was right, that she would see Marcus soon, and still alive.

✳✳✳

Carter and Maria waited by the airport security checkpoint as planned. They anxiously waited for Sophia to arrive.

"There she is!" Maria waved frantically to get her sister's attention.

The two sisters embraced and started to cry.

"How is Jose?" Sophia asked.

"He did well overnight. I'm sure he'll be thrilled to see your face when he wakes up this morning," Maria replied.

Carter stood in silence, shocked at who he saw standing in front of him. He finally spoke, "Hi, Sophia, it is good to see you again."

"Carter, is that you?" Sophia asked in amazement.

"When Jose told me his mother's name was Sophia, memories of my spring break in Belize came back to me, but I never imagined you were the Sophia he was talking about. The one I fell in love with."

Sophia blushed.

"We have a lot of catching up to do, but first I must get you to the hospital and Marcus someplace safe. Maria will fill you in on the events from last week."

Carter hurriedly escorted Sophia and Maria to the hospital. Jose's condition continued to improve. He was starting to show signs that he was waking up. Carter hated to go and was hoping Jose would be more alert. He left Sophia holding Jose's hand while encouraging him to wake up. On his way out he touched base with the FBI agent standing guard. "Has anyone tried to visit Jose?"

"A police officer stopped by and wanted to question him. I told the officer that Jose was not allowed any visitors and would be unconscious for several more days."

"Good. Don't let anyone in to see Jose no matter what they tell you. They can't be trusted. We need to keep Jose in ICU until he's well enough to move. Rosa will be back this evening to relieve you." Carter glance back at the ICU door.

The agent could see the concern on Carter's face and his hesitancy to leave. "Don't worry, they're in good hands. I won't let anything happen to them."

Carter knew what laid ahead wasn't going to be easy to pull off. He couldn't delay any longer. It was time to put his plan in motion.

Carter stopped by his place to quickly shower and change clothes. He drove to Rosa's apartment, worried that Marcus may have changed his mind and left. He hoped Marcus didn't have second thoughts about his plan and take off while he still could. He knocked on the door quietly knowing Rosa was inside resting. He was relieved when Marcus cracked the door to let him in.

"Are you ready to go?"

Marcus held out his hands so he could be cuffed.

Carter loosely cuffed his hands behind his back. "Do you have any questions before we leave for the police station?"

"No. It's in God's hands now."

Carter agreed he was going to need divine intervention to pull this off. He said a little prayer under his breath.

They arrived at the police station and Carter escorted Marcus inside. As soon as he entered the squad room with Marcus in cuffs beside him, a hush fell over the room. He paraded Marcus past the captain's office, on purpose, on the way to the interrogation room. Then he waited in anticipation to be accosted by his captain. Before he could sit down the captain entered the room and asked to speak to Carter in private. Carter stepped just outside the door. Before Carter could say a word the Captain started in on him.

"I thought I took you off this case?"

"You did sir, but Marcus contacted me this morning and wanted to turn himself in. What was I supposed to do, tell him to go back to Belize, that I was no longer on the case?"

"So what has he told you so far?"

"Nothing yet. I plan to interview him now before booking him to see what he knows."

"I'm going to assign another officer to take his statement."

"Maria, his wife, told him that I could be trusted. He won't talk to anyone else."

"Okay, I'll let you do this one last thing on the case but I'm going to send another officer in with you to make sure you don't screw this up."

118

"You can count on me sir, I've got this."

The captain turned and left without another word. Carter figured he planned to returned to his office and contact Dragone to share Marcus' location. Carter entered the interrogation room and was joined by another officer. He wondered if the officer was another pawn of Dragone's.

The interview went as planned and Marcus detailed his involvement with the drugs and money exchange in hopes of getting Jose back. He was booked on drug and kidnapping charges. Before Carter could place Marcus in a cell, the FBI appeared right on schedule.

Carter watched as the captain tried to convince the FBI that they were overstepping their boundary and that they had no jurisdiction over the case. Of course they weren't taking it, and explained that kidnapping was a federal crime. They would be taking the prisoner and handling the case from here on out. The captain realized defeat and watched as Marcus was escorted from the station, still in handcuffs, by the FBI.

The transport went as planned. Once inside the FBI vehicle Marcus' handcuffs were removed. He was provided a wig and cap to wear to hide his identity. Marcus managed to jump out of the vehicle at the first turn as planned. He raced inside the parking garage and found the waiting dark green van. Carter slid open the passenger door and he jumped inside. He slumped down in the back seat before he could be seen.

"Long time no see," Carter tried to joke to lighten the mood. "Stay down. I'm going to wait a few minutes to make sure the coast is clear before we leave and disappear from the face of the earth." Carter pulled down his baseball cap to conceal his image from any cameras before driving away.

✳✳✳

The cream colored stucco safe house appeared at the end of a sand road. It was just enough off the beaten path to not raise suspicion. Cameras were strategically placed around the perimeter of the property, so no one could approach without being seen. The house had been stocked with supplies to last several weeks so there would be no need to leave.

"I know it's not the Hilton but this place will keep you alive." Carter opened the front door and searched the house to make sure they were alone. "Make yourself at home. Alex should be here shortly to take over guard duty."

Marcus placed his few belongings in the back bedroom.

"Would you like a soda?" Carter yelled from the kitchen.

"Sure," Marcus replied.

They both made themselves comfortable in the family room and Carter turned on the television. *"This is a Breaking News Alert!"* was the first thing they heard. Carter turned up the volume.

"The fire department responded to a house explosion on Azalea Avenue. The cause of the explosion is currently unknown. One person was found dead inside. No identification has been provided by the authorities. Stay tuned for the six o'clock news for an update."

"Well, Dragone didn't waste any time. Tomorrow the identity of the body found will be confirmed as you. Don't worry, no one was hurt. The FBI used a John Doe that they have had in storage for several months."

Marcus sat in stunned silence.

"You okay?" Carter asked.

"I know you said he would try to kill me, I just never thought he would act so quickly. Are you sure that Maria and Jose are safe?"

"When Jose wakes up the doctors are going to report that he suffered a brain injury. That when he was shot, he experienced a blow to the head that affected his memory. His memory may never return. Hopefully that will convince Dragone he's no longer a threat. Jose, Sophia, and Maria will be escorted back to Belize along with your supposed body. We'll use Teo's body in your place. I'll stay with them until the trial is over to make sure they stay safe."

"Then what, will we ever be free from this? Even if my testimony puts Dragone away for many years, his men will still be free to do his dirty work for him. You don't honestly think that prison will stop him from getting revenge for my testimony. He'll just have one of his goons hunt me and my family down." Marcus ran his hands through his hair. "I should've never agreed to this."

"I know everything looks bleak right now. But I'll find a way for you to be safe. You have to trust me."

Marcus hesitated before speaking. "I may have a way to help my situation. I left out a piece of my story after Teo made the drug and money exchange."

"I'm listening."

"On the way to your place to pick up Jose, Teo made a stop first.   He went to a storage unit and opened one of the compartments. He said he rented the unit under a fake name so no one could trace it back to him. When he opened the door the space was filled with old furniture. Teo said he bought cheap furniture at garage sales so no one would suspect the unit was being used to store money. Teo stepped over some run-down chairs and sofa until he reached the very back of the unit. He stopped at an old military style storage trunk. He unlocked the trunk and opened it. I was amazed at what I saw. It was almost full of cash. Teo crammed in most of the half million dollars he had just received. Then he closed and relocked the trunk. Teo said that was his retirement plan so he could marry his girlfriend and get out of town."

"Do you remember where this storage unit was located?"

"It was dark but I think I can find it again."

"Did Teo ever mention his girlfriend's name?"

"No, but I know he talked to her on his cell phone, so her number should be in his phone."

"The FBI has his cell phone so I'll check with Alex and see what I can find out. You think this money may be your answer for starting a new life and keeping your family safe?"

"Yes, that's my thought."

Carter sat quietly while he decided how to proceed. He knew any money received during the exchange of drugs could be confiscated by the police. But at the same time he understood that Marcus' family could definitely use the money. He rationalized that after what Marcus was willing to risk to put Dragone behind bars that he deserved the money. "Okay, this is what we will do."

***

A car approached the safe house just after 3AM. Carter drew his gun and held it by his side. He stared at the camera images transmitted on the computer screen. He waited to confirm it was Alex, his friend with the FBI, before opening the door. The familiar face appeared across the screen. Carter blew a sigh of relief. He secured his weapon and unlocked the door.

"Has everything been quiet here tonight?" Alex asked.

"Yes, only a few deer, raccoon, and an armadillo wandered by the camera."

"Good, just the way I like it."

"Were you able to catch the men that blew up the house that Marcus was supposedly in?"

"They launched a couple of pipe bombs through the windows of the safe house, then they tried to escape in their vehicle. We had them surrounded before they got ten feet away. They were taken away into custody before any emergency personnel arrived. Obviously our story to the authorities is that they got away. They've been in interrogation ever since and the last I heard they were starting to crack."

"Good, maybe we can tie them to Dragone. Alex, I would like you to meet Marcus."

"Marcus, glad to meet you. I'm guaranteeing you'll make it to trial in one piece."

"I appreciate your help in protecting me and my family."

"Carter, why don't you get some rest and let me get acquainted with Marcus?"

"Yeah, I could use a few hours. I need to hook up with Rosa later and check on Jose."

"Understand, no problem. I'm here until the trial is over."

✳✳✳

Carter woke just after 10AM, still feeling like crap but knew he had too much to do to sleep. He found Alex on the computer in the kitchen. Marcus was still asleep. "Any update before I leave?"

"Not really, but the pieces are starting to fall into place. I talked to Marcus for several hours and he was very helpful. We should have plenty of evidence to put Dragone away for the rest of his life."

"I'll be on the down low until I see you at the trial. You have my burner phone number if anything changes," Carter said before leaving.

Carter drove to his place before heading to the hospital. The long days were starting to take their toll. He looked in the mirror and rubbed the stubble on his face. He showered, shaved, and found a pair of clean beige slacks and hunter green cotton short sleeve collared shirt. He added some fresh bird seed and water to Rosco's dish. "Sorry Rosco, I know I've been neglecting you lately." Rosco danced up and down, trying to entice Carter to pick him up. "Not today bud, I've got to run. I'll see you in a few days. You try to stay out of trouble." Carter turned on Rosco's favorite radio station to keep him company while he was gone. Country music blared from the radio. Carter smiled at Rosco as he joined in.

"She don't give a damn…," Rosco sang, bobbing up and down and dancing to the music.

Carter locked his front door and checked to make sure he wasn't being followed before heading to the hospital. He walked into the ICU and found Rosa sitting outside of Jose's room. "How's he doing today?"

123

"Unbelievably well. The doctors are amazed at his progress. He's alert, eating, and talking," Rosa responded.

"Has he shared anything with you on where he has been the last couple of days?"

"No, I'm not pushing him. I want to give him a chance to get stronger and enjoy being reunited with his mom. He has been asking for you," Rosa said.

"Really?"

"Why do you sound so surprised? You know you made a connection with him. Why else would he tell Father Michael that you were his dad?"

"Don't remind me, that was another time I let him down."

"Nonsense, quit feeling sorry for yourself." Rosa never hesitated to tell Carter how she really felt.

Carter prepared himself for what he might see when he entered Jose's room, and put a smile on his face. "How are you doing, buddy?"

"Carter, you came! I've been telling Mama all about you and how you took care of me."

Carter looked into Sophia's tired eyes and saw nothing but gratitude. "I think I could've done a little better job, but I'm glad we found you when we did."

"Mama says I will be returning to Belize in a few days. Will you come to visit?"

"I might do better than that. I have some vacation time coming to me. I thought I might stay with you for a few weeks." He didn't tell Jose the real reason he would be visiting was to protect him.

"Oh boy, I can show you around my neighborhood! You can meet Nana and my cousins."

Maria spoke up, "My two boys are staying with their grandmother while I'm here. Did everything go as planned with Marcus?"

"Yes, everything went prefect." Carter looked back at Jose. "You concentrate on getting your strength back so you can get out of here. I've got to get back to work but I'll see you again real soon. Maria, can I talk to you outside for a minute?"

They stepped into the waiting area where Rosa was standing guard. Carter discussed his transportation plans with them. "Maria, I know this is going to be difficult for you but you have to pretend that Marcus is dead. As soon as the doctor allows Jose to leave we will fly back to Belize. A coffin will be boarding the airplane with us with Teo's body inside. We are going to pretend it's Marcus, though. You will plan Marcus' funeral and bury him when you get home. We have to keep up the charade to keep Marcus safe."

"I understand and I'll throw the best funeral ever for Marcus. None of his friends will suspect anything. You can trust me."

"Good. I'll be there with you in case there are any hiccups. Obviously, you'll have a closed casket, since Marcus' body was burned beyond recognition."

Maria started to laugh. "Marcus would love this. He always enjoyed playing practical jokes on his friends and family. This is going to be the biggest one yet. We're going to have to record his funeral for him so he can see it at a later date."

Carter was glad Maria could find some humor in all of this. "Now that Marcus' funeral is settled, let me find Jose's doctor and determine when he can be released."

Carter returned a short time later to discuss the exit strategy with Rosa. "The doctor feels that if Jose continues to improve at his current rate, and there are no unforeseen complications, he should be well enough to travel in two days with some restrictions. I'll start making the flight arrangements and keep you posted."

"Sounds like you've got everything under control. I'll stay here as many hours as I can to keep the police away from Jose."

Carter left the hospital and drove to the precinct. He went directly to his captain's office to request vacation, to start immediately. The captain was more than happy to accommodate him to keep Carter away from the Dragone investigation, or so he thought. Carter returned home to pack for his vacation and start making travel arrangements to get everyone back to Belize safely. Everything was going as planned.

***

Three days later Carter, Jose, Sophia, Maria, and Teo's casket with Marcus' supposed remains all boarded the plane in Miami headed for Belize.

"Can I sit next to the window, Mama?" Jose begged Sophia.

"Of course." Sophia loved seeing the excitement back in Jose's eyes. She felt like she had failed him. He never would've left if he had been happy at home. She did the best she could with Jose growing up without a father.

"Carter, will you sit next to me?" Jose asked eagerly.

"Sure, if your mother doesn't mind."

Sophia smiled and nodded to let him know it was okay. She moved over to the aisle seat and swapped places with Carter. Maria's seat was on the other side of the aisle next to Sophia. Sophia felt strange seeing Carter again after all these years. It brought back so many feelings she had buried many years ago. They hadn't had any time alone since she had arrived. She had so many questions for him. She wanted to know what had happened to him after he left Belize, why he never tried to contact her, and if he had ever married.

The plane started to accelerate down the runway. Carter noticed Sophia holding onto the arm rest for dear life and realized how scared she must be. He grabbed hold of her hand to reassure her.

Once at altitude Jose was mesmerized by the vast ocean below and the fluffy clouds slowly floating by. "Have you ever flown before?" Jose asked Carter.

"I have a few times," Carter laughed, thinking of the many times he traveled by aircraft for pleasure and business. He remembered his first time flying with his dad when he was only five years old. His dad had received his private pilot license and

126

purchased a used Cessna 172. This was a time in Carter's life when he was still close with his dad. They spent time together in the evenings and weekends. It was before the business had taken off.

"Why does it look like we are moving so slow?"

"It's just an illusion due to our high altitude. I guess traveling back to Belize is much better than the way you arrived in Miami?"

"Definitely!" Jose laughed.

"Do you feel up to telling me what happened to you after you left my place?"

Jose thought for a little while as if trying to remember. "I stayed with a lady and her kids the first night. Then I walked to a church where I met this nice priest who let me paint some furniture in his office. He served me the best lunch I think I've ever tasted. It was ham and bean soup with corn bread."

"You must've been pretty hungry." Carter laughed. "Where did you go after lunch?"

"There was a school just down the road with children about my age out front. They were loading the school buses so I got in line with the rest of the kids and followed them onto the bus. I made friends with a boy who sat next to me. He asked if I wanted to go home with him, since his parents were still at work. He lived in an enormous house. You should've seen it!" Jose said full of excitement as if it was the adventure of a lifetime.

"Did you spend the night with him?"

"No, it started to get late and I didn't want his parents to see me and start asking questions. I pretended to live in the neighborhood and told him I needed to get home," Jose said sadly.

Carter felt bad for Jose being all alone with no one to take care of him. "You must've been scared?"

"No, not really. It wasn't long before I saw a delivery truck. When the driver wasn't looking I sneaked in the back and covered myself with a tarp so he wouldn't see me."

Carter was amazed at how intuitive Jose was. "So where did you spend the night?"

"I slept in the truck. The next morning I quietly exited the truck before anyone could see me. Once outside I discovered I was near the airport. I thought I might be able to catch a flight home. I road a shuttle bus from the airport parking area to the terminal. When the bus stopped I got off and made my way to where the airplanes were boarding."

"How did you get past Security?"

"When they were distracted I walked past," Jose said as if it was no big deal. "Then I ran into Aunt Maria."

"I bet you were surprised to see your Aunt?"

"Was I ever! She took me to a restaurant. I had a big hamburger and a milkshake."

"That sounds awesome." Carter knew the rest of the story from there and didn't push him to remember his experience with Dragone or when he was shot. Carter could tell Jose was getting tired and was fighting to stay awake. "Why don't you lean your head against my shoulder and try to get some rest?"

Jose didn't argue. He was sleeping soundly in just a few minutes.

While Jose slept, Carter took the opportunity to talk to Sophia. "Jose tells me you work in housekeeping at a hotel."

"Yes, I do that and clean some of the vacation homes in the area."

"When I last saw you, you were talking about going to college and studying to be a nurse. What happened to that plan, if you don't mind me asking?"

"I got pregnant and had to take care of my baby."

"What about Jose's father, was he ever in the picture?"

"No, the father didn't want anything to do with the baby," Sophia sadly shared.

"I'm so sorry. I wish I had kept in touch with you like I promised. Once I got back to Miami life took over and I was busy finishing my senior year at college."

Sophia looked down toward the floor so Carter wouldn't see the hurt in her eyes. "There was nothing you could've done."

"Well, I'm here now. I'm going to make sure you and Jose stay safe until the trial is over. I'm not going anywhere soon."

"My house is very small. I don't know how comfortable you'll be staying there," Sophia said.

"Believe me, I'm used to roughing it and can sleep in the car if I have to." Carter reminded Sophia, "This isn't a vacation." He whispered in her ear in case Jose was listening, "I'll need to stay alert to make sure no one tries to take Jose again."

They landed without incident. Carter was given a Chevy Trax at the rent-a-car office. It had enough room for all of them and their bags. Jose directed Carter where to go as they left the airport. Belize was as Carter remembered it, with the endless sunny skies, crystal clear waters, white beaches, and lush green terrain. It was just a little more crowded than the last time he had visited. There were many more hotels and condos built along the beach. They weaved their way through the side streets as Jose pointed the route to his house.

It wasn't long before Jose yelled, "There it is!"

A small light green wood framed house on concrete blocks with a small front porch came into view. Beautiful yellow hibiscus were blooming along the front of the house. Carter knew how much Sophia loved flowers. He stopped the car and turned off the engine. He could still hear the jets taking off from the airport in the distance. He remembered Jose telling him he lived near the airport.

Everyone exited the vehicle and started to gather up their bags. Before Carter could unload his Jose grabbed his hand. "Let me show you my room!"

Carter was pulled toward the house. He was amazed at Jose's resilience. He seemed to have already put what happened to him out of his mind. "Slow down, buddy. What is your rush?"

They were greeted by an older lady at the door. "Hello there, young man. I'm sure glad to see you. You better give your Nana a hug." She leaned down and hugged Jose tightly. "Child, you better never run away again. You almost gave me a heart attack."

"I'm sorry Nana. I promise I won't."

"Hi, I'm Carter," he introduced himself.

"Nice to meet you Carter." She hugged him tightly, welcoming him to their home. "Thanks for watching out for my grandson."

Jose grabbed Carter's hand once again. He anxiously pulled him toward his room. "This is my room. I collect model airplanes. I assembled these all by myself." The airplanes were placed in a row on a shelf attached to the wall above Jose's bed. Jose picked up each airplane and told Carter their names. There was everything from a P-51 Mustang to a yellow Piper Cub.

"Wow! That is quite impressive. I didn't know you were into airplanes."

"Yeah, I want to be a pilot one day and travel all over the world."

Carter thought to himself, I hope that dream comes true for you.

"I know my bed is small, but you can sleep on it and I can sleep on the floor."

"No buddy, I'm not going to kick you out of your bed. You need your rest to get well. I'll work something out with your mom. Don't worry, I plan to stay close to you. How does that sound?"

Sophia popped her head in the room. "Jose, you've had a long day. Nana has fixed us all something to eat. Then I want you to go right to bed."

"Oh Mama, can't I stay up a little longer? I slept on the airplane."

Carter spoke up. "I'll be here when you wake up. You can finish showing me around then."

After supper Sophia tucked Jose in bed and sat with him until he fell asleep. She crept out of his bedroom and left the door ajar. She wanted to be able to hear him in case he needed anything. She joined Carter on the front porch outside.

"I know you are blaming yourself for Jose running away, but I can tell you're a wonderful mother. Boys will just be boys sometimes though. There was nothing you could've done to stop what happened to Jose."

Tears came to Sophia's eyes. She had been staying strong for Jose the last several days and exhaustion had taken over. She couldn't hold back the tears any longer. Carter reached to console her. He embraced her gently. "It's all right. I know how scared you must've been for him. He's safe now."

Sophia pulled herself away from Carter. She wiped the tears from her face, embarrassed for losing control in front of him. "You're right, I'm just tired and need some rest, as I'm sure you are. Why don't you stay in my bed and I'll sleep on the sofa?"

"Nonsense. I'm not going to run you out of your bed. Help me move the sofa into Jose's bedroom, that way I can sleep near him."

Sophia was too tired to argue. She helped to quietly maneuver the sofa near Jose's bed. She handed Carter a pillow, sheet, and light blanket.

"If you need anything I'm right next door," Sophia whispered.

Carter made himself comfortable on the sofa. He took out his laptop and waited for it to boot up. He brought up a Miami news link. A trial date had been set for Dragone. In three weeks he would have to return to Miami to testify.

✳✳✳

The next morning Carter woke to the wonderful aroma of coffee and banging in the kitchen. The sun had not yet lightened the sky. He looked over at Jose, who was still sleeping soundly. Carter quietly eased from his bed and slipped into the kitchen.

131

"I hope I didn't wake you," Sophia said. "I couldn't sleep and baking eases my mind."

"The smell of that wonderful coffee woke me. I forgot how much I missed the strong Belize blend."

Sophia poured him a mug full. "Do you still take cream and sugar?"

"I'm trying to watch my waistline and just take cream now," Carter joked. He took a sip and smiled with pleasure. "Oh, this is heavenly."

"You must be used to some pretty bad coffee," Sophia laughed.

It was good to hear her laugh. It brought back memories of the times they had spent together on the beach during spring break, without a care in the world for a whole week. "I'm glad we have this time alone. I want to apologize for never contacting you after spring break as promised. When I started back to college I was thrown back into the real world. I thought of you often but never tried to reach you. For that I'm terribly sorry. You deserved better."

Sophia didn't want Carter to see how disappointed she was by his actions. "I knew a wealthy boy like you would soon forget about a plain girl like me and go on with your life. I didn't really expect to hear from you again," Sophia lied to cover her hurt.

"You make me sound so shallow. The wealth was my father's, not mine, and he disowned me when I didn't follow in his footsteps after college."

"Did you ever marry and have children?"

"No, work always seemed to get in the way of a steady relationship. After the police academy I worked hard to get upgraded to detective. The hours didn't allow much of a social life. What happened to you after I left? You had such dreams for yourself."

"I finished high school soon after you left. Then I became pregnant, so I had to think of my baby. My family didn't make much money as farm workers and I couldn't ask them for help. I found a job cleaning hotel rooms and rental homes. I was able to

132

save enough to rent this house. My father died shortly after Jose was born. Mom and Maria moved in with me. Mom helped take care of Jose while I was at work. Maria married Marcus when Jose was two and moved next door. It has been a blessing to have my sister and mom so close."

"Jose said his father was dead. What happened to him?"

Sophia looked at her clenched hands and hesitated for some time before answering.

Carter could tell she was struggling to answer the question. He stayed silent and gave her time to get her thoughts together. Being patient and not filling the void by talking was something he had learned during interrogations. Nine times out of ten the person would eventually speak and answer his questions.

"When we slept together that last night you were in town I thought I loved you."

Carter forced himself to not speak so Sophia could finish.

"No one had ever treated me like you did. I didn't own nice clothes or live in an expensive home. You saw past that, though, and treated me like I was special and that I could do anything with my life. I had hoped the fantasy would continue, but after you left life returned to normal for me also. I had to help my family in the fields and finish school. That summer I started getting nauseous working in the hot fields. When the nausea persisted I went to the doctor. He informed me the nausea wasn't due to the flu but from me being pregnant. I told Jose his father was dead because I was too embarrassed to tell him the truth, that I became pregnant after sleeping with a man I had only known for a week, who I never heard from again." Sophia blinked back tears.

Carter grabbed her hands, still clenched in front of her on the kitchen table. "Are you trying to tell me that I'm Jose's father?"

"Yes."

Carter couldn't believe his ears. "Why didn't you contact me? I would've been here in a minute to take care of you, if I only knew."

"I had no way to contact you. By the time I knew I was pregnant, you had graduated from college and moved."

Carter realized what she said was true. He hadn't given her his phone number or his parents' address. In fact, she knew very little about him other than he was a rich kid having fun during spring break his senior year in college. "I'm so sorry Sophia that you had to go through this alone. I should've contacted you once I returned to the states. I resumed college and before I knew it I was studying for finals and trying to decide what I was going to do after I graduated. My Dad wanted me to join his financial investment business but that wasn't what I wanted. I wasn't interested in spending my days in an office talking to clients. I wanted to make more of a difference in this world. I thought being a cop would give some meaning to my life, so I joined the police academy as soon as I graduated. My Dad disowned me and we haven't spoken since. After four years as an officer I was able to pass the detective exam and started working in homicide. When Jose told me he was from Belize you immediately popped into my head. The fun we had together and the love you showed me; I haven't found that kind of love since. I missed what we had together. But not in my wildest dreams did I think Jose had anything to do with the spring break we spent together. I don't know if you can ever forgive me for deserting you like that to raise Jose on your own. I have grown very attached to Jose and hope you'll let me be part of your lives."

"I never blamed you for what I got myself into. I'm not saying you didn't break my heart, just I was very young and I let my infatuation for you get the best of me." She looked up and smiled.

Carter squeezed her hands and stared into her big brown eyes. She had not lost any of her beauty during the last twelve years. She was still just as gorgeous with her slender, petite figure, long silky brown hair streaming down her back, and smooth, bronze skin. "You have done an excellent job of raising Jose on your own. I have never known a smarter, more resilient eleven year old boy. Remember, I was a boy once. I tried to get away with all kinds of things on a daily basis without my parents finding out. I know I can't make up for lost time but want to be a part of your life if you will allow me."

Jose walked out of his bedroom before Sophia could answer. "Hey buddy, how are you feeling this morning?" Sophia asked.

"A little sore." Jose held his stomach.

"That's understandable after the long journey yesterday," Carter added.

"How about I make you some pancakes with honey?" Sophia asked.

"Oh boy, that's my favorite! Will you have some with me?" Jose asked Carter.

"I think I could manage to eat a few pancakes myself this morning," Carter responded.

After breakfast Sophia left for work and Carter kept Jose company in his bedroom while he rested. Jose told him about his school, playing soccer, how hot it was working in the fields in the summer time, and the stories went on and on for a while until Jose fell asleep, all talked out.

Carter watched him sleep peacefully and felt like the luckiest man in the world to have Jose as his son.

Eleven

A week passed and Carter hadn't noticed anything suspicious that might make him worry about Jose's safety. He wasn't taking any chances, though. He kept Jose inside the house to give him a chance to heal from his wounds and stay out of sight. He didn't want to give Dragone an opportunity to hurt Jose again. The trial was still two weeks away and so far Marcus was still presumed dead.

Jose was allowed out of the house just long enough to attend Marcus' funeral. It was held at a Catholic church just a few miles from their home. The closed casket, located in the front of the sanctuary, was draped in beautiful red roses. The ceremony began with the priest blessing Marcus and bringing peace to everyone by letting them know that Marcus was in a better place. Then Marcus' many friends got up one by one to speak. They shared stories about him, some funny and some serious. They described what a difference he had made in their lives. Carter realized what a truly good man Marcus was after hearing all the good he had done. He had impacted so many lives of the people around him.

Maria spoke last, putting on a good act. "Marcus was a loving husband and father." A tear ran down her face as she continued. "He always put his family's needs before his own. His two sons are blessed to have had such a wonderful father and the lessons he taught them about life will live on with them forever. He will be greatly missed." There wasn't a dry eye left in the packed church. Marcus would've been proud if he could have heard his memorial.

After the service the house was flooded with well wishers and tons of food. Carter stayed close to Jose to make sure he was safe and didn't overexert himself. He could tell the long day was taking a toll on him.

136

"Are you feeling okay?" Carter asked.

"My stomach is a little sore."

"Here let's get you in bed. You may have overdone it today." Carter walked next door with Jose and tucked him in bed.

Carter made himself comfortable on the sofa. "Don't worry, I'll be here when you wake up."

Jose stared up at the ceiling. "Have you ever thought about dying?"

"In my line of work it is kind of hard not to."

"Do you think my dad can see me from heaven?"

Carter hadn't expected that question. Sophia had asked Carter to not tell Jose the truth about him being his father until he was stronger and his wounds had healed. Sophia was scared he would be angry with her and run away again. "I believe we still have some connection with our families after they pass. I remember when I was about your age, my Papa, the name I called my grandfather, passed away. He used to take me fishing almost every weekend. My own father was always too busy with work. We would fish until there was no more bait and the sun was going down. After he passed I went to our old fishing hole at a lake near my home. I stood along the shore with my line in the water. I hadn't been there long when a buck walked down to the water's edge for a drink. I stood perfectly still watching the deer as he sipped from the lake. After the deer had quenched his thirst, it looked right at me with it's big, brown eyes. The deer stared almost as if he recognized me. I was entranced by his penetrating stare and wasn't the least bit afraid. The deer didn't run away, but turned and made himself comfortable, lying down in the dry leaves, in the cool shade underneath a large oak tree. It felt like my Papa was sitting there with me fishing, keeping an eye on me."

"I hope if you die you will still watch over me."

"You don't have to worry. I'm not going anywhere." Carter felt bad for Jose. He had seen way too much death in his short life.

Jose succumbed to his exhaustion and fell asleep. Carter listened as all the people paying their respect next door slowly left.

He quietly left Jose's bedside in search of Sophia. He found her doing dishes in the kitchen. "Let me help. You must be exhausted." Carter reached for the sponge and took it from Sophia's hand.

Sophia smiled up at him. "Is Jose resting soundly?"

"Yes." Carter hesitated before he proceeded. "Jose asked me a question about his father. He wanted to know if he could see him from heaven."

"What did you tell him?"

"I told him yes, I felt he could, but I didn't like deceiving him. I think we should tell him the truth tomorrow. I don't want to lose his trust."

"Your're right. I've hidden the truth from him for too long. First, let me explain to him why I lied. Then we can tell him together how we met and why you have been absent from his life."

***

The next morning Carter woke to the sounds of hammering. Jose was still asleep so he quietly left his room to investigate the cause of the noise. The house was eerily quiet. He walked outside and found Sophia and Maria talking to their neighbor. The sky was bright orange as the sun started to crest over the horizon. "Hey, what's with all the noise this morning?"

"There is a storm coming. The neighbors are boarding up their windows to protect them from flying debris."

"How big of a storm are we talking about?"

"The hurricane is up to 155 mph and is headed straight for us. It should hit tonight," Maria said.

"Why haven't we heard about this before now?" Carter asked.

"It intensified quickly overnight from a tropical storm into a major hurricane."

Carter took control. "What can I do to help? Do you have any lumber to protect your windows?"

"Yes, Marcus always keeps some wood stored in his shed behind our house," Maria spoke up.

Carter followed Maria next door and peered inside the shed. Sheets of plywood were stacked along the wall. With Maria and Sophia's help they moved the plywood out of the shed. They took a sheet at a time and securely nailed the pre-cut boards over the windows. Both houses were protected from the approaching storm by 9AM. Sweat was pouring off Carter's brow and his face was beet red.

"You look like you're about to pass out," Sophia said. "How about we take a break and get some cold water?"

"That sounds like a good idea." They retreated inside to cool off before finishing. They still needed to pick up the loose items outside around the house that might become flying debris in the storm.

Carter leaned over the kitchen faucet and splashed water on his face and neck to remove the sweat. Sophia handed him a towel. "We make a good team. How have you managed all these years by yourself?" Carter asked.

"I had Maria and Marcus to help me when needed." Sophia handed him a large glass of ice water.

Carter took a big gulp. "Oh, that is just what I needed."

"How about I fix us some breakfast before it gets any later? I'm surprised Jose isn't awake yet with all the noise we've been making."

"Let me check on him while you start breakfast. There's no way he could have slept through all that racket," Carter said with a bit of concern in his voice.

"Jose has always been a deep sleeper. It's just about impossible to get him up for school."

Carter peeked into Jose's room. Jose was wrapped in several blankets even though it was a very warm morning. "Hey buddy, are you feeling okay this morning?"

There was no reaction from Jose. Carter placed his hand on Jose's forehead. He was burning up. He scooped Jose into his arms and ran back to the kitchen. "We've got to transport Jose to the hospital! He's burning up and I can't wake him."

Carter gently placed Jose in the back seat of his rental car with Sophia cradling his head. He raced through the streets honking his horn as he flew past the other cars on the road. He pulled up to the emergency room, lifted Jose out of the back seat, and ran inside. "I need help! My son is unconscious and is running a high fever!" Carter yelled.

Hospital personnel quickly showed Carter to an exam room. He placed Jose gently on the table. Sophia and Carter watched while the doctor examined Jose.

The vital signs were relayed to the doctor. "Pulse is weak, blood pressure is 90 over 52, fever is 104."

Carter explained to the doctor, "Jose was shot about two weeks ago and has been recovering at home. He complained of stomach pains last night but I just thought he had overdone it at his uncle's funeral."

"Let's get a scan of his stomach and see what's going on."

Jose was quickly wheeled away. Sophia and Carter were left alone in the room. "I thought the worst was over now that we were home. He was doing so well. I don't understand," Sophia said through her tears.

Carter gave Sophia a hug. He felt so helpless. Then he had an idea. "Wait here for the doctor to return. I need to make a few phone calls. I'll be right back."

Carter stepped outside and called his parents. "Hi, Mom."

"Carter is that you? It's been years. How are you doing?"

"I'm fine, but I need Dad's help. Is he available?" Carter hadn't spoken to his father in at least ten years.

"You know your father. Even though it's Sunday he had just a few things he needed to do at the office. What's this about?"

"I don't have time to explain right now. I'll give him a call at work. I promise I'll call again soon so we can catch up."

Carter quickly ended the call and dialed his father's office number. Even though he hadn't talked to his father in years, he still remembered the phone number. He would call his father most evenings after school to tell him about his day. His stomach tensed as he listened to the phone ring. He anxiously waited to hear the familiar voice answer.

"Hello."

"Dad, it's Carter."

"What do you need? I know you must need something or you wouldn't be calling."

Carter bit his tongue and tried to keep his anger at bay. "As a matter of fact I do. I can't explain everything right now but you have a grandson that is currently in the Belize hospital. He needs to be transported to Miami Children's Hospital today or he might die. Would it be possible to send your corporate jet to pick us up and take us to Miami before the hurricane hits tonight?"

"You had a kid and you never even bothered to call to let me and your mother know?"

"Dad, I just found out myself about a week ago. Like I said, I can explain everything when I get back to Miami. Time is of the essence. Can you help?"

"Of course. I have two pilots on standby. They should be able to get to Belize in a little over two hours."

"Thanks Dad. You have no idea how much this means to me. I'll call you once we arrive in Miami."

Carter walked back inside and found Sophia talking with the doctor.

"It appears there may be a small nick or tear in Jose's intestine that is leaking bowel into his stomach. We have started him on some strong antibiotics to try to stop the infection from spreading. We have also administered a drug to help bring down his fever."

Carter interrupted the doctor. "Is he strong enough to fly back to Miami to be treated at the Children's Hospital located there?"

"He's currently stable. His blood pressure has risen a little and his fever has come down slightly. He's in and out of consciousness because of the medicine we gave him. To answer your question, yes I think he's strong enough to make the trip to

Miami today. But I wouldn't delay. He needs immediate medical attention to repair the tear and constant supervision until he's out of danger."

"With the hurricane approaching, could we get an ambulance to take us to the airport within the next two hours?"

"Yes, I can find you someone to help arrange that."

"Great! There should be a jet waiting for us at the airport when we arrive. Let me know what you need from me to arrange transport."

The doctor showed them to the administrative offices where they completed Jose's release paperwork and documentation to transfer him to an ambulance.

Sophia's mind was racing, trying to catch up with what was going on. Finally, all the paperwork was complete. Carter took Sophia by the hand. He led her to his rental car and handed her the keys.

"I need you to pack up everything you can't live without and be back here in an hour. Also, tell your mother, Maria and your nephews to do the same."

"Carter, you need to explain to me what is going on before I move another step."

Carter could tell Sophia was upset. "I'm sorry, I didn't have time to run this by you first before I made the arrangements. My father is sending his corporate jet to pick us up and take us to Miami. With the hurricane quickly approaching we don't have much time before the weather will make it impossible to leave. We'll all be much safer if we get out of the path of the storm. I know the doctors in Miami and they can provide Jose with the best medical treatment. I'll stay here with Jose. Now go quickly! Return with your family and their belongings before it is too late!" Carter looked up at the sky and the clouds were becoming more menacing by the hour.

Sophia realized she had to trust Carter in order to save Jose. "I'm putting my faith in you, so don't let me down. I'll be back shortly," Sophia said as she got into Carter's vehicle and raced away.

Twelve

The jet ride out of Belize was a little bumpy at first, but once over the ocean the air smoothed out. Sophia relaxed and released the death grip she had on the arm rest. Jose slept through the entire trip. Once on the ground in Miami, they were expedited through customs. Jose was taken by a waiting ambulance to the hospital. The doctor that performed Jose's surgery after being shot was standing by. Carter's father had arranged a limo service to take the rest of them to the hospital. They arrived at the hospital as Jose was being prepped for surgery. They looked like refugees carrying all their belongings, wearing crumpled clothes and exhausted stares.

Sophia kissed Jose on the forehead with tears in her eyes. She told him, "I love you. Stay strong my little one. I'll be here when you wake up."

They tried to make themselves comfortable in the waiting area. They had no idea how long Jose would be in surgery. Carter asked, "Can I get anyone some coffee or food?"

Sophia wasn't hungry but Maria knew her boys were probably starved. Maria left with her sons and mother to find the cafeteria.

Carter tried to reassure Sophia, "He's a strong kid. He'll pull through this."

"I just keep going through my head that I should have seen signs that Jose was unhappy and done something to prevent all this from happening to him," Sophia said.

"Believe me, there is nothing you could've done to have foreseen this. I remember when I was eight years old, I was mad at my dad for not making it to one of my baseball games. He broke many promises when I was growing up. To punish him I decided I was going to run away. I packed my backpack and hid in my best friend's tree house. I stayed there until after dark when I had decided I had punished my parents enough. I walked home expecting to find them frantic with worry and thrilled to see me. I arrived to an empty house. My Mom had a charity event that night and my Dad was still at work. Mom had left me a note on the refrigerator that there was some leftover spaghetti for me to eat. The note instructed me to heat it in the microwave for two minutes. They didn't even know I was missing."

"That must've been horrible for you!"

"I was obviously disappointed my plan hadn't worked. But I got over it. Kids are very resilient. Jose running away is a normal fantasy for boys his age. There is nothing you could've done to stop him. Jose just made it a little further than I did."

"Well, I'm going to make sure it doesn't happen again. I'll do whatever it takes to make him happy."

"Maybe I can help with that by being in his life." Carter leaned over and kissed Sophia on the forehead. "I'm not going anywhere this time."

Sophia rested her head on Carter's shoulder. He comforted her by placing his arm securely around her shoulders.

Maria returned a short time later with her sons and mother. The boys were tired after their long journey. They laid down on a sofa in the waiting area. It wasn't long before they were both asleep with their heads in their mother's lap.

Carter excused himself to make some phone calls. He called Rosa first to let her know he was back in town. He wanted to hear the latest news about the case.

"Hi, you miss me yet?" Carter asked jokingly.

"How is Jose?"

"He developed an infection and we're back at the Miami hospital. He's in surgery now."

"Oh no, that's not what I wanted to hear."

"How's everything going at your end?" Carter asked.

"The FBI gathered enough evidence against the captain and four other officers to arrest them for racketeering, hindering the investigation of a federal case, and helping a fugitive to escape.

They recorded the captain's conversation after Marcus was arrested and heard him tell Dragone where Marcus was supposedly being held. That connected him with the fire bombing at the safe house and Marcus' death. The captain won't be back any time soon. Dragone's trial is scheduled to start in about a week."

"Good, I'm ready to testify and put Dragone behind bars for a long time. How's Rosco doing?"

"That bird of yours is driving me nuts. Every time I come home I'm greeted by *Bang, bang! Get down!* He's lucky to still be alive!"

"Yeah, that takes some getting used to. Thanks for taking care of him for me. I've one more favor to ask."

"You got it. What do you need?"

"This evening I need to leave for a few hours. Can you stay here at the hospital with Sophia and Jose to make sure no one tries anything?"

"Of course. I'll plan to leave work at five and will head that way."

"Thanks! I don't have to remind you not to tell anyone we're back in town."

"Mums the word. I never heard from you." Rosa said.

Carter ended the call and realized for the first time how much he missed work. The thrill of putting the puzzle pieces together to solve a case, and the satisfaction he received from catching the bad guys and putting them behind bars are what drove him. What was he going to do when all of this was over? After ratting out the captain and several officers he knew he wouldn't be welcome back in the department. He now had someone other than himself to consider. He had to think about what would be best for Jose and Sophia. They deserved that much from him.

Carter called Alex next. He said little just in case his phone was being monitored. "Are you enjoying your fishing trip?"

"Yes, but haven't caught much in the way of fish."

"Are you up for some company?" Carter asked.

"Sure, as long as you come the back roads, the main road is under construction."

Carter understood that Alex just wanted to make sure he wasn't followed. "No problem. I'll arrive around midnight."

Carter returned to the waiting area. There was still no word on Jose's condition. He, along with everyone else, was starting to worry. The hours passed and Carter became concerned that Jose may not pull through.

Rosa arrived as promised. "How's he doing?"

"There hasn't been any news yet," Carter said.

Rosa joined them in the waiting room. She paced with Sophia while they waited for news from the doctor.

Finally, the doctor appeared from behind the closed doors. "I'm sorry to keep you waiting. The surgery took longer than expected but I wanted to make sure I wouldn't have to open Jose up again. The nick in Jose's intestine was successfully repaired. His system was thoroughly flushed to help the infected tissue heal. I inspected the area to make sure there was no more damage. He did very well. His vitals are strong. He is currently in recovery. You should be able to see him in about an hour."

Tears of joy and relief came to Sophia's eyes. Carter gave her a reassuring hug. "Rosa is going to stay with you tonight." Carter looked over at Maria. "I thought you might like to visit your husband."

"Really, we can see him? It won't put him in any danger, will it?"

"No, I've made the necessary arrangements with Alex. He's expecting us."

Carter borrowed Rosa's car and left with Maria, her sons, and mother. He drove north on 95 and watched as the bright lights of Miami disappeared behind him. The safe house was located in a remote area off 95. Carter kept a watchful eye to make sure no one followed them. No headlights exited with them off the interstate. It was almost midnight and the rural road was deserted.

He pulled into the driveway of the safe house and flashed his headlights so Alex would know it was him.

Maria woke up her sons to let them know they had arrived at their destination. The boys were eager to see their father. They ran into the house, followed closely by Maria. Carter had never seen such joy. The boys wouldn't let go of their father. He embraced them all as the tears flowed.

Carter unloaded all their belongings. He touched base with Alex before leaving the jubilant family reunion to return to the hospital. The car seemed quiet. This was the first time he had been alone in weeks. Thoughts of his parents entered his mind. He had forgotten to call them when he arrived in Miami. Even though it was after 1AM, Carter knew that his Dad would be awake. "Hi, Dad. Sorry to call so late. I just wanted to thank you for sending your jet. Jose made it through surgery and is in recovery."

"Your mom and I were talking. We would like to meet our grandson and put the past behind us."

"I would like that very much. Jose doesn't know yet that I'm his father." Carter proceeded to explain how he and Sophia had met and how they were reunited. "Sophia and I plan to tell Jose about me as soon as he's well enough. Let me get through the trial next week and make sure Jose isn't a target. As soon as I know he's safe and strong enough, I'll arrange for you to meet. I know you'll love him as much as I do."

Carter ended the call and a sense of peace fell over him. It was good to have his parents back in his life again. He was going to be part of a family again and hadn't realized how much he missed that. He arrived at the hospital just after 2AM. He found Rosa and Sophia asleep in their chairs by Jose's bed. Jose had several tubes protruding from his arms and laid motionless. Carter quietly woke Rosa so she could go home. He followed her outside the room so as not to disturb Sophia or Jose. "Has anyone tried to visit Jose?"

"No, all has been quiet other than the nurse checking on him every hour or so."

"Good. Thanks again for your help and use of your car." Carter handed Rosa her keys.

"No problem. Keep me posted. Don't hesitate to call if you need anything," Rosa said as she left.

Carter returned to Jose's bedside. He collapsed in the chair previously occupied by Rosa. He studied Jose's small, innocent, frail body. He wanted to be the father to Jose that he had never had. He hoped he could have what he witnessed tonight with Marcus and Maria; a family who stood by each other no matter what.

✳✳✳

The next day, to the joy of Carter and Sophia, Jose opened his eyes and asked where he was. Through tears of elation Sophia explained the jet ride back to Miami and what had happened.

"Boy, I can't believe I missed the jet ride!" Jose said with disappointment in his voice.

"I'll have my father take you up again real soon once you are well," Carter explained.

"Your father has an airplane?" Jose asked.

"Yes he does, and I'm sure he would love to take you for a ride as often as you like."

The doctor arrived and was glad to see Jose alert and talkative. "Looks like our patient is doing well. His temperature and vital signs appear normal. How do you feel, Jose?"

"I'm a little sore." Jose pointed to his tummy.

"That's understandable. I'll tell the nurse to give you some more pain medicine. It'll help with your discomfort and let you rest."

"When should he be able to leave the hospital?" Carter asked.

"If he continues to improve he should be able to go home in a couple of days to recuperate from there."

The doctor left and Sophia reminded Carter, "I'm not sure we'll have a home to return to after the hurricane last night."

Carter spoke up. "You can stay at my place for as long as you need."

"Oh boy! Mama, Carter has the neatest bird that talks," Jose exclaimed.

Sophia smiled up at Carter. "Jose, there's something I need to tell you. I haven't been perfectly honest with you about your father being dead."

Carter reached for Sophia's hand. He held it tightly to give her the courage and support she needed to proceed.

"I had you when I was very young and I didn't know how to contact your father after you were born. I told you he was dead because I thought it would be easier on you. I didn't want you to think you weren't loved by your father. I met Carter when he visited Belize his senior year in college. He returned to the states and then I discovered I was pregnant with you."

"Carter is my father?" Jose interrupted.

"Yes," Sophia replied.

Carter couldn't hold his tongue any longer and spoke up. "I'm so sorry I haven't been there for you, but I'm hoping you and your mother will stay in my life now that we have found each other again. Would you like that?"

"Would I! We can play baseball together and you can watch me play soccer."

"I would really like that." Carter could tell Jose was getting tired. "But first you need to get well. Why don't you rest for a while? Your mother and I will be here when you wake up. Then we can plan everything we're going to do together when you get out of the hospital."

Jose didn't argue and was asleep again within a matter of minutes. Carter turned on the television in the room with the volume down low so as not to disturb Jose. He searched until he found the weather channel. Damage from the hurricane was being broadcasted as the storm continued to strengthen and head

150

toward the panhandle of Florida. The aerial photos of Belize were heartbreaking. Sophia recognized what was left of her neighborhood. Pieces of homes were scattered everywhere. There was no way her house had survived.

Carter asked Sophia, "Would you consider starting a new life here with me in Miami? I know I can't turn back time. I'm not the same selfish college student you met twelve years ago. I've a lot of time to make up for and want you both in my life."

"I'm not the same innocent girl you met on the beach. I put up a wall around me after you left. I vowed to never let myself get hurt again by another guy. My sole focus has been on taking care of Jose. I can't make you any promises about our future but I want you in Jose's life. I know that's what's best for him."

Carter wanted more than just friendship from Sophia but knew he had to take it slow. He didn't want to hurt her again. "Just let me take care of you for a change and we'll see where it goes?" Before Sophia could answer, Carter's cell phone rang. The only people that knew his burner phone number was Alex and Rosa. He answered it immediately.

"We've been made. Everyone is safe. I'm on the move. Be on the lookout. You may be next," Alex alerted Carter.

Sophia looked into Carter's eyes and saw the fear.

"Understand," was all Carter said in response.

"We have to get out of here," Carter told Sophia.

"Jose is in no condition to travel," Sophia said.

"I'll arrange everything. Stay here with Jose and don't let anyone into the room. Not the doctor or nurse. Do you understand?"

"Yes."

"I'll be right back."

Carter disposed of his burner phone in one of the hospital rest room garbage cans and found a phone in the lobby to use. He called his father. "I have another favor to ask. Do you still have the condo on the beach that your clients use?"

"Yes."

"Good. I need to move Jose immediately. Our current location is no longer safe."

Carter's father knew about Jose's situation with Dragone and understood. "What can I do to help?"

"Do you have a medical friend that you would trust with your life?"

"Yes."

"Meet me at the condo with your doctor as soon as possible."

Next, Carter contacted Rosa. He told her, "Our location is no longer secure. I need you to rent a van using a fake name and pull around the back entrance to the hospital as quickly as possible."

"Understand. I'll be there in thirty minutes."

Carter returned to Jose's room with a wheelchair. "How's he doing?"

"He is sleeping soundly," Sophia said.

"Good. Rosa is on her way to pick us up. My Dad is going to meet us at his condo with a doctor to take care of Jose. I'm going to gently remove Jose's IV and hopefully not cause him any additional pain. Then I'm going to lift him into this wheelchair. When the coast is clear we are going to sneak out of here without anyone seeing us." Carter lifted Jose's feather light body and carefully placed him in the wheelchair.

Sophia wrapped a blanket snuggly around him to keep him warm.

"Okay. Now I need you to check to make sure the hall is clear," Carter said.

Sophia peeked her head out the door, looking both directions. There was only one nurse present at the nurse's station and she was busy on the computer. She motioned for Carter to follow. They made it to the elevator without being stopped. Sophia pressed the down button and the elevator door opened immediately. They hurried inside and pushed the button for the lobby. When the door opened they walked casually to the back exit. Rosa waited with the van door already open to load Jose in the back. Sophia quickly got in and Carter eased Jose onto her lap. Carter jumped in the passenger seat. He made sure no one saw them leave. Rosa pulled away from the curb and joined the flow of traffic as she exited the hospital. Carter instructed her where to drive. She drove slowly, trying to avoid any bumps that might cause Jose pain. Carter glanced over his shoulder and was glad to see Jose was still sleeping soundly. He only hoped he had enough drugs in his system to keep his pain at bay until they could reach the condo.

The condo complex came into sight. Rosa pulled up to the security gate and Carter told her the code to enter. The gate swung open. She drove to the delivery entrance. Carter got out and carefully lifted Jose from Sophia's grasp. He carried him to the freight elevator. They took the elevator to the top floor and exited. Carter's father was waiting for them to arrive. He motioned for them to enter his condo.

"Come right in here. I've set up the master bedroom for Jose and Sophia."

Carter gently lay Jose down on the large, plush bed.

Sophia pulled the covers over Jose and snuggly tucked him in bed.

"Carter, I'd like you to meet Dr. Carmel. He's an old friend and will keep our confidence. You don't have anything to worry about."

Jose opened his eyes.

"Are you doing okay, buddy? I had to move you while you slept."

"I'm very sleepy."

"It's okay. Go back to sleep. Your Mom and I are here with you."

"Let me have a look at you before you go back to sleep," Dr. Carmel said.

"Jose, Dr. Carmel is going to take good care of you and help you get all better," Sophia reassured Jose.

Dr. Carmel lifted Jose's batman pajama top and examined his incision. He gently pressed around Jose's stomach. "Tell me if this hurts," the doctor instructed Jose.

"Just a little," Jose said.

"Good. Let me listen to your chest. Can you breathe for me?" Jose took a deep breath.

"Is there any pain?"

"Not much."

The doctor continued to examine Jose and took his vital signs. "He seems to be doing very well for a boy that just got out of surgery twenty four hours ago. Based on what you told me about his procedure I'll need to keep a close eye on him. I'll give you some pain medicine to administer as needed and antibiotics to prevent any infection. I'll stop by in the mornings and evenings to check on him. But if he starts running a fever or complaining of any pain, call me immediately." He handed Carter his home and office numbers. "Make sure to give Jose plenty of fluids so he doesn't get dehydrated. He should be able to eat soft foods like soup and Jello without it upsetting his stomach."

"You have no idea how much I appreciate this," Carter told the doctor. "As I'm sure my father has told you, no one is to know we're here."

"Yes, he explained your situation. You have nothing to worry about. I'm a widower so no one will question my unexpected trips."

"Dad, this is not how I planned for you to meet your grandson."

"Nice to finally meet you, young man." He shook Jose's small hand. "I hope we'll get to spend some more time together soon."

Carter, his dad, and Dr. Carmel left the bedroom so Jose could get some rest. Sophia made herself comfortable in the bed next to Jose. She wanted to stay close in case he needed anything.

Carter walked the doctor to the door. "Thanks once again for your help."

"No problem. I'm glad I could help. Jose seems like a very special boy. Like I said, don't hesitate to call."

"Dad, I have one more favor to ask before you leave. I would like you to meet Rosa, my partner."

"I'm glad to finally meet you." He shook Rosa's hand.

154

"You too, sir. Your son has saved my backside more than once," Rosa said.

"Dad, can you take Rosa to her car so I can stay here with Jose?"

"Of course. I'll stop back by tomorrow to see how Jose is doing, if that's all right?"

"You're welcome to stop by any time. Bring mom so she can meet Jose. Keep your eyes open for any strange people or cars around work or home. I don't know what length Dragone may go to stop me from testifying."

"Will do. I'll tell your mother to stay close to home until the trial is over. I'll have security in my building and around our community keep an eye out for any strangers. Don't worry about us. Just take care of our grandson."

His father beamed with pride. "Oh, before I leave, your Mom loaded me up with food from the refrigerator. Just heat it up when you get hungry."

"Tell her thanks for me. Rosa, call me if there are any new developments on the case. Stay alert. I don't know to what lengths Dragone will go to save his ass."

Rosa and his Dad left. Carter securely locked the dead bolt behind them. He peered into Jose's room and was glad to see Jose was back asleep. Sophia laid next to him, sleeping soundly. Exhaustion had finally caught up with her. Carter quietly closed the door. His stomach was reminding him that he couldn't remember the last time he had eaten. He opened the refrigerator and spied some delicious looking lasagna and a large bowl of salad. He heated up a little of the lasagna in the microwave and put some salad in a bowl. He was hungry, but picked at his food. He had more pressing concerns on his mind. Would Dragone discover their new hideout?

Thirteen

The following week Dr. Carmel arrived each morning and evening as promised. Jose was doing great. His wound healed nicely and there were no further complications. Carter was going stir crazy though, hiding out in the condo all week. He was beyond ready for the trial to be over. He hadn't heard from Alex and hoped they were somewhere safe and hadn't been discovered yet. The trial was set for the next day. Rosa was the only one that had his new burner cell phone number and was asked to notify him when it was his turn to testify.

The call came three days later at 8AM. Rosa informed Carter, "You and Marcus are scheduled to testify today. I will be by shortly to pick you up." A short time later, a knock at the door alerted Carter to Rosa's arrival.

"You have no idea how glad I am to see you! If I had to stay in that condo one more day I think I might go nuts," Carter said.

"Jose, it's so good to see you up and about," Rosa said. "I brought a few games for us to play while Carter is gone."

Jose grabbed the bag out of Rosa's hand to see what was inside. He spread the items out on the table to examine each one. "Oh, boy! A Battleship Star Wars game. I've been wanting this one."

"It sounds like you have your afternoon planned for you!" Carter laughed. He knew Rosa would keep them safe in his absence. "Jose, have fun with Rosa while I'm gone."

Carter looked into Sophia's eyes and saw the worry. "I'll be back before you know it." He kissed her gently on the lips.

"Be careful," Sophia said. They had grown much closer after being confined in the condo together.

Carter left with some apprehension. He hoped Rosa hadn't been followed and their location was still safe. Once in the parking lot he looked around for any strange vehicles. He got in the van Rosa had rented for him and drove off. He pulled over once out of sight of the parking area and exited the vehicle. He ran back to the condo parking area and concealed himself behind a palm tree. He watched the building for fifteen minutes. He wanted to make sure none of Dragone's men entered the building after he had left. He was satisfied no one was going to surprise Rosa. He made his way back to the van, then drove to the courthouse without incident.

Carter entered the courtroom and found a seat behind the prosecuting attorney. He looked around and didn't see Alex or Marcus. A girl was called to testify and walked up to the stand. He recognized her immediately. She was one of the young girls, whose hands were bound behind her back on the boat. He could only imagine what she had gone through. It was very difficult for her to give her testimony. She told the jury about being drugged and then used to entertain Dragone's guest during a party on the boat. The details were hard to listen to. By the time she was finished she was in tears. There wasn't a dry eye on the jury. The defense didn't even try to cross-examine her. The damage had already been done to their case.

Carter was called next to the stand. He was asked to relay his account of events leading up to Jose's kidnapping. He explained that he had received a tip that Jose was being held at the address given for the condo. When he arrived to rescue Jose, gunfire erupted. Jose was injured in the crossfire. The prosecution finished with their questions. It was the defense's turn next. The attorney tried to place doubt in the juror's minds about Carter's testimony.

"Did you actually see Dragone with your own eyes at the scene?"

"No, but a witness did."

Carter was cut off before he could continue. "No further questions, your honor."

Carter stepped down from the witness stand, feeling bad that his testimony hadn't gone as well as planned.

The prosecutor stood up to address the judge. "Your honor, I have one final witness but need a short break before calling him forward."

The defense jumped up. "Your honor, we've heard from everyone on the prosecution's witness list. I wasn't made aware of this new witness. I haven't had time to prepare my cross-examination and this witness shouldn't be allowed to testify."

The prosecution had anticipated this argument. "Your honor, this witness was just made known to me this morning. That is why it wasn't disclosed to the defense sooner. An attempt was made to kill my witness to keep him from testifying. I didn't want to jeopardize his safety once again."

"I will allow it, but you have thirty minutes to produce the witness or we'll go to closing arguments."

"Thank you, your honor," the prosecuting attorney said.

Carter followed the prosecuting attorney out of the courtroom. "Is Marcus somewhere close?" Carter whispered as they quickly walked toward the prosecutor's office.

"I don't know."

"What do you mean you don't know? Haven't you been in contact with someone from the FBI to let them know that Marcus would be testifying?"

"Even the FBI have been kept out of the loop as to where Marcus is being held. I have no idea if he's even still alive or if he knows he is scheduled to testify today."

The prosecutor picked up the phone and urgently talked to someone on the other end, trying to find out if Marcus was on his way. The prosecutor slammed down the phone in frustration. "They think he's on his way. They are standing guard at the entrance of the courthouse to protect him when he arrives."

There was only five minutes left before the deadline. The attorney opened the door to his office to return to the courtroom. An old man approached him.

Carter recognized the eyes. "Marcus, is that you?"

"Yes, Alex made me wear this disguise so I could enter the courthouse without being seen."

"Hurry, we have just enough time to get you to the courtroom to testify," the attorney said.

Marcus hurriedly removed his wig, beard, and glasses. Alex appeared out of nowhere.

"Good to see you, man. I was starting to think they got to you," Carter said as he slapped Alex on the back.

"Ye of little faith," Alex said.

Marcus was surrounded by Alex, Carter, and the attorney to protect him from any unexpected assailants. They made it to the courtroom without incident and hurried inside to meet the deadline.

"You are cutting it very close," the judge announced as they entered.

"I'm sorry, your honor. My witness is ready to testify."

Marcus took a seat on the stand. He took a deep breath to calm his nerves. He glanced toward Dragone and all he saw was evil penetrating from his eyes.

The prosecution began, "Marcus, could you please tell the court how you came to know Dragone?"

Marcus took his time and explained how his brother smuggled and sold drugs for Dragone. The jury listened intently as he continued. He told the jury about how his brother died and how he was contacted to deliver the million dollars in drug money in exchange for Jose. He explained in detail how Dragone was not satisfied after receiving the money and how he ordered his men to kill him and Jose. As Marcus finished, there was total silence in the courtroom. Everyone was stunned by the gripping testimony.

It was finally over. The jury took only four hours to come back with a guilty verdict on all charges. Carter was elated and relieved. There was much congratulatory handshakes with Alex and Marcus. They watched as Dragone was lead from the courtroom in handcuffs. His sentencing hearing was scheduled in three weeks. With the verdict the judge had no option but to sentence him to spend the rest of his life in prison.

Fourteen

Once outside the courthouse Carter pulled Marcus aside. "How are Maria and your family holding up?"

"Better than me. They've been real troopers, staying inside and out of sight."

"I know you want to get back to them to share the good news, but thought you might want to make a stop first."

"Okay, what did you have in mind?"

"Get in." Carter opened the van door for Marcus and started driving. "Do you remember telling me about Teo's storage unit?"

"Yes."

"Can you lead me to it?"

"I think so. It was dark but only a few blocks from your apartment building."

Carter drove to the general area and Marcus pointed out the streets to turn on. Rows of storage units came into view.

"Where to now?"

"It is unit 193."

Carter slowly made his way down the rows until he reached the one labeled 193. He came to a stop. Marcus got out and tugged on the door. It was securely padlock. "I don't have the key. How are we gong to open it?"

"No problem." Carter pulled a crowbar from underneath the drivers seat. He broke the lock and removed it, then slid open the door. "Presto! Just remember, I was never here." Carter pulled his baseball cap down to conceal his face from any cameras.

Marcus climbed over the old, dusty furniture to the back of the unit. He found the trunk that Teo had opened that night, which seemed like ages ago. He used the crowbar to break the latch. He slowly opened the lid, wondering if he had imagined what he had seen inside. It was still there. The trunk was full of money.

Carter threw Marcus a duffel bag. "You deserve this after everything you've gone through. This is your chance for a fresh start. You'll be able to take care of your family."

Marcus and Carter quickly filled the bag full of money, then Marcus zipped the bag closed. He struggled to lift the heavy laden bag and carry it over the old furniture. Carter closed the storage unit door and they returned to the van.

"Now what?" Marcus asked.

"Now you have some decisions to make. Do you want to return to Belize and rebuild your house, destroyed by the hurricane, or would you like to start a new life here?"

"Staying here is an option?"

"I'm sure after risking your life to put Dragone behind bars, the FBI might be willing to help you receive a visa to remain in the United States."

"I have to talk to my family first, but I've always wanted to own my own farm. Do you think this would be enough money to do that?"

"I think we could probably make that work!" Carter laughed to see Marcus smiling after such a long time. "I have one more thing to share with you."

"What is it?" Marcus asked.

"Alex provided me the name, phone number, and address for Teo's girl friend, Alecia. She works as a bartender at one of the fancy restaurants on the beach. Would you like to visit with her before returning to the safe house?"

"Teo was looking forward to marrying her." Marcus looked at the bag full of money. "I know he would want her to have some of the money. Would it cause problems if I gave her one hundred thousand dollars from the money we collected?"

"That is awful generous for someone you've never met!"

"I know if Teo loved her she must be someone special."

"We would just have to make sure she understood that the money couldn't be placed in a bank account, or the IRS might start asking questions. Also, there is the matter of Teo's vehicle still parked at Rosa's place. She gave me the keys today and verified the registration is in Teo's name. Now that we have his death certificate you can have it transferred into your name if you like."

"I totally forgot about Teo's Nissan Altima. Can we pick it up after we meet Alecia? If I'm going to stay in this country I will need a vehicle."

"Yes. Once you get settled into your new home we will get the title transferred." Carter drove to the address Alex provided for Alecia's apartment complex. Marcus counted out the money and placed it in a brown paper grocery bag Carter had left in the van. He folded over the top of the bag to seal it so no one would see what he was carrying. They approached the door to the apartment number given to Carter and rang the bell. A beautiful, tall slender tan woman with sun bleached hair opened the door.

Carter spoke up, "I'm Detective Carter with the Miami Police Department. Are you Alecia?"

"Yes I am. Is this about Teo?"

"I would like for you to meet Marcus, Teo's brother."

A smile brightened her face. "Teo talked a lot about his older brother. It's so nice to meet you. I've been following the trial. I'm glad you were able to put the man behind bars that killed Teo."

Marcus finally spoke. "Teo also told me about you. He was looking forward to marrying you. Teo wanted me to make sure you received this if anything ever happened to him." He handed Alecia the bag full of money.

Alecia looked inside and her eyes said it all. "I can't accept this. I'm sure Teo's family needs this more than I do." She handed the bag back to Marcus.

Marcus understood why Teo loved this woman so much. She put his family first before herself. "You don't have to worry, Teo also provided for his family. Please take this. I know he would want you to have it so you could use the money to buy yourself something nice."

Alecia hesitated before taking the bag. "My parents house was damaged during the last hurricane and this would go a long way to repairing the roof. Thank you for your generous gift."

"Before we leave, there is just one more thing. Teo stored this money in a safe place to use for your wedding and to start a life together. He showed me the location in case anything happened to him. Don't try to deposit it in a bank or it may raise suspicion."

Alecia met Carter's eyes and was surprised at his reaction. He didn't seem to have an issue with where the money originated. "I understand. I'm not one to go on a big spending spree. I'll use it sparingly to help my family so no one will question where I received it."

"I'm afraid I have to break up this reunion. Marcus has to get back to his family before it gets any later," Carter said.

"And I have to get to work. Thank you so much for taking the time to stop by so I could meet you. Your brother had a good heart. I will miss him dearly."

***

Carter stopped by Rosa's apartment just long enough for Marcus to pick up Teo's car. Marcus followed Carter back to the safe house. There was a round of cheers and kisses when they arrived. Carter pulled Alex aside. "Do you think Marcus will be safe now that Dragone is in prison?"

"That was my hope, but seeing how persistent Dragone was to kill Marcus before the trial I wouldn't put it past him to try again. He may want revenge now that the trial is over."

"Have you talked to Marcus about going into a witness protection program?" Carter asked.

"I made him aware of that possibility. I'll discuss it further with him and his family after I make a few phone calls."

"What about Sophia and Jose, do you think they are safe?"

"Knowing how Dragone operates, if his men can't find Marcus they'll find anyone close to Marcus and make them suffer for what he has done."

"I was afraid you were going to say that. I have something to confess."

"What is it?"

"After Jose was shot, I discovered I knew his mother, Sophia, from my college days. Do you remember that senior trip we made to Belize?"

"I was pretty drunk the whole time we were there. I barely remember it," Alex joked.

"Well, Sophia and I became very close that week, if you know what I mean. She told me Jose is my son."

Alex stood there in stunned silence. "You're kidding me, aren't you?"

"No, I'm not. I slept with Sophia before I left Belize and then never talked to her again until now."

"What are you going to do?"

"I'm not sure, but it sounds like if I want to be a part of Jose's life I might have to disappear with them to keep them safe."

"Have you ever considered putting in for a job with the FBI?"

"I haven't really thought about it. You think they would be interested in hiring me?"

"I'm sure with everything you did to help put Dragone behind bars, and a recommendation from me, they would hire you in a second. Maybe I could find you a job in one of our branch offices in Atlanta. We can relocate Marcus' family along with Sophia and Jose to that area under a new name."

"Marcus expressed interest in owning his own farm. He recently inherited some money from his brother Teo." Carter looked away from Alex. He didn't want to give away how Marcus came across the money.

"This money that mysteriously appeared. Would it have anything to do with Teo's occupation?" Alex asked.

"I have no way of knowing where the money came from, just that Teo wanted Marcus to have it if anything happened to him."

"I see. Well, I'm sure Marcus is grateful for Teo's generous inheritance. I agree he deserves it after everything he has been through."

"My thoughts exactly."

"We need to move everyone as soon as possible. Is Jose well enough to travel?" Alex asked.

"Yes, he's doing much better. He'll love to go on a trip and see something other than the walls of the condo. I'll talk to Sophia tonight when I return to the condo to convince her that this would be best for them. I can have their things packed tomorrow morning and meet you back here. I trust you'll keep Marcus's family safe until I can join up with you."

"I won't let anything happen to them," Alex assured him.

"I have to stop by the police department and resign, then close up a few loose ends here before I leave."

"Send me your resume as soon as possible so I can start the process of getting you hired with the FBI. Marcus' family will no longer exist after tomorrow. I'll see if I can locate a farm outside the Atlanta area where they can reestablish their lives."

"Thanks Alex. I owe you big time for this," Carter said.

"It's me that owes you. Getting Dragone off the streets didn't hurt my reputation any. Be careful and watch your back," Alex said. "We'll plan on leaving as soon as you arrive with Sophia and Jose tomorrow and before our hideout is discovered."

***

Carter arrived at the condo a little after midnight. He knew everyone was probably asleep so he quietly opened the door and stepped inside. He saw Sophia asleep on the sofa with the television turned down low. The next thing he felt was a gun pressed against his temple.

He looked over at the person holding the gun. "It's just me," Carter said

"Carter, you scared the crap out of me! Why didn't you call to let me know you were returning tonight?" Rosa asked.

"Sorry, it was late and I didn't want to wake you."

The noise woke Sophia. She looked up at Carter and smiled. "You did it! We saw them take Dragone away in handcuffs after the verdict was read on the news tonight. He didn't look too happy."

"Yes, Marcus did an excellent job of testifying. There was no way the jury could find him innocent after all the evidence was revealed."

Sophia hugged Carter. "I'm glad this is finally over."

"Well, not quite yet. Why don't you both have a seat? Alex and I have a plan going forward to make sure Dragone doesn't get one of his men to retaliate for him."

"What do you mean? I thought once Dragone was behind bars we could go on living our lives without fear."

"That was what I was hoping. Since Dragone has been so persistent with trying to kill Marcus, Alex feels prison won't stop Dragone from trying to hurt Marcus or his family. Alex is processing the paperwork to assign you and Jose a new identity, along with Marcus' family and your mother."

"What about you?" Sophia asked. "You're in just as much danger as we are."

"I'll also be getting a new identity and moving with you to somewhere outside the Atlanta area. Alex is trying to get me a job with the FBI so I can work in the Atlanta bureau. That way I can stay close to you and Jose."

Rosa looked tired and sad. "I'll miss you, partner. Things will be boring without you around."

"I'm sure the new captain will want to replace me as soon as possible. You'll probably be the lucky one and get to train the new guy."

167

"Who's to say it won't be a woman," Rosa laughed. "Wouldn't that be great, to have two women detectives on the force?"

"I don't know if the force could handle all the estrogen!" Carter joked. "Thanks for always having my back. I plan to stop by the precinct tomorrow to resign."

"Make sure you see me before you disappear for good," Rosa said as she left.

Sophia hadn't said a word. They were now alone. "You have been awfully quiet. Do you think you could adjust to life here in the states?"

"I obviously want what's best for Jose," Sophia said.

"I'll make sure we get him in a good school. What about you, what do you want?" Carter asked.

"I'm not sure."

"At one time you wanted to be a nurse. If that's still your dream, here is your opportunity to go to college and become one. If you want to be a housewife I'll be more than happy with that also."

"Sounds like you already have us married."

"I know we haven't had much time to get to know each other again. These last few weeks you've reminded me of what I left behind and what a fool I was to have not stayed in touch with you. Once you get settled into your new home I would like to take you on a real date. Let's just see where it goes. I won't pressure you, and we can go at whatever pace you are comfortable with."

Sophia blushed, "I would like that."

"Tomorrow morning we'll share the news of our new life with Jose. Then we need to pack and meet up with Alex by noon. I want you out of the Miami area as soon as possible before Dragone discovers where you've been hiding. Try to get some rest. Trust me, it'll all work out."

***

168

The next morning Sophia and Carter shared with Jose that they would be traveling to Georgia. They hoped to find a nice town and home for them to establish their new residence.

"Oh boy! Does that mean you'll be staying with me and Mama?"

"Yes, I hope to live with you or at least very near you once we get relocated."

"Will you take me to a baseball game?"

"Let's first get moved and settled into our new home, Sophia said, beaming brightly at her son. We have to find you a school before the new school year begins. Carter is going to be very busy with his new job and we don't want to take up all of his time."

"I'm looking forward to spending a lifetime with you, but right now we need to pack up everything and get on the road," Carter interjected.

Sophia's and Jose's sparse belongings didn't take long to load into the van. Jose chatted all the way to the safe house. He was so excited about his new adventure. They arrived just before noon to the cheerful greetings of Marcus and Maria. Maria and Sophia hugged and tears started to flow again. Alex had to break up the reunion so they could leave.

Carter walked over to Sophia and gave her a hug. "I'll see you soon." He kissed her on the forehead. Then he wrapped his arms around Jose and lifted him in the air. "Stay close to your mom and be good." He set Jose on the ground.

Carter watched with a sense of emptiness as they drove away.

Carter entered his apartment with his arms full of boxes to start packing the few things he planned to take with him. Before he could set the boxes down though, he felt a gun pressed up against his temple. This time it wasn't Rosa.

169

"What took you so long?" the man asked as he pushed the door closed behind Carter. "Now you're going to give me your gun and not do anything stupid."

Carter slowly placed the boxes on the floor. Another man stood in front of him with a gun pointed in his direction. Carter carefully slid his gun out of the holster.

"Hand it here!" the guy in front ordered.

Carter reluctantly released his weapon.

"Good. Now have a seat on the sofa where I can keep an eye on you."

Carter sat and lowered his hands to his sides. "What do you want?"

"I'll ask the questions. You're going to tell me where I can find Marcus or you'll be sorry."

"What do you plan to do if I don't tell you, kill me?" Carter laughed. "I know whether I tell you or not you plan to shoot me."

Carter was slapped across the face with the butt of the gun, causing his upper lip to bleed. "Like I said, we can do this the hard way or I can see how much pain you can tolerate first."

Carter knew he needed to buy some time. "I don't know where he is. The FBI has Marcus in a safe house somewhere. They didn't tell me where they placed him."

Whack! There was another blow across Carter's face, this time breaking his nose. "You better find out where he's located or I start breaking fingers."

"Okay, let me call my contact with the FBI and see if I can get him to tell me." Carter pulled out his cell phone and called Alex.

"Put it on speaker so I can hear," the gunman ordered.

"I didn't expect to hear from you so soon, is everything all right?"

"Yeah, just peachy. I have some items that Teo left for Marcus. Can you give me the address to the safe house where he's staying so I can deliver them to him?"

Alex realized Carter was in trouble and that his conversation was probably being monitored. "Sure we're using the house just outside West Palm Beach. Do you remember how to get there?"

"Yeah, I remember. I should be there in a little over an hour." Carter disconnected the call, hoping that would give Alex enough time to have someone waiting at the house to ambush these guys when they arrived.

"So what is the address to the safe house in West Palm Beach?" the gunman asked.

"I don't know the exact address. It's off the highway a ways. You have to take a few back roads and then it is located at the end of a sand road. It's a safe house. It's not like it's located in a subdivision. I'll have to take you there."

The guys were not at all pleased with this information. Carter was finally able to convince them that this was the only way to find Marcus. One of the gunmen saw the packing tape Carter had brought with him.

"Bind his hands in the front using this." The gunman threw the roll of tape to the other guy.

Carter reluctantly held out his hands in front of him. They were tightly bound almost to the point of cutting off his circulation.

"Now we're going to walk to my vehicle. Don't try any funny business."

A gun was jabbed into Carter's side. They made their way slowly to the parking lot. They approached a black SUV with dark tinted windows, similar to what Teo had driven. "Get in the back!" Carter was shoved inside.

One gunman joined him in the back seat while the other went around to the driver's side door. They headed north on 95 in silence. As they approached West Palm Beach, the driver asked, "Which exit do we take?"

"Take the highway 441 exit."

He turned off the highway. "Left or right?"

"Turn left."

They headed west. "How far?"

171

He wasn't a man of many words, Carter thought. "In about five miles, you'll turn right onto a sand road that runs along the canal."

They reached the canal. The sand road wasn't in the best of shape. "You better not be steering me in the wrong direction," the gunman warned.

"No, it's just a little further down this road." They bumped along for another mile. "Turn left here."

They approached the safe house. There was a car parked in front. Good, Carter thought to himself. Someone was waiting for them.

The black SUV came to a stop with a dust cloud engulfing them. The gunmen didn't move. "I don't like this. Why is no one coming out to greet you?"

"They don't recognize this vehicle. I'm sure they are just being cautious," Carter replied. He knew he had to get away from them before they figured out they were being ambushed. With his hands still taped he quickly lifted his legs and kicked the gunman next to him in the face hard. He rapidly opened the passenger door and hit the ground running as fast as he could away from the vehicle. Shots rang out as he dove for cover behind a bush.

The shooting finally stopped.

A man's face stared down at him. "Alex sent us. Do you need an ambulance?"

Carter looked down at the dried blood on his shirt. He realized what his face must look like after the abuse it had taken. "No, I'll be fine. Thanks for coming."

The two gunmen were hauled away in body bags while Carter explained what had happened. He was finally allowed to leave, and was offered a ride back to his apartment. It was now after dark. He knew it wasn't safe to stay the night. He splashed water on his face and changed his bloodstained shirt. Then he quickly stuffed the contents of his closet in a box, placed it in the rental van he was still driving, and drove away, knowing he would never be back. Exhaustion had set in and for the first time in a very long time he wanted to go home to the place where he had been raised.

He made sure no one had followed him as he approached his parents' house. It was just like he remembered it. The manicured lawns, large palm trees lining the driveway, brightly lit entrance leading to the etched glass of a flamingo on the front door. Carter hadn't called his parents to warn them that he was coming. It was now after midnight, but he knew his Dad would still be up.

He rang the doorbell in anticipation of being scolded like when he was a child. The door opened and his Dad stood there wearing a robe and slippers.

"Sorry to disturb you so late, but could I stay here tonight?"

"Who is it darling?" Carter's Mom appeared behind his dad.

Before Cater could say another word his dad grabbed his arm and led him inside. His mom's face said it all. I must look like death after what I have been through, Carter thought to himself. He was so glad to finally return home.

Fifteen

Carter woke the next morning more rested than he had been in weeks. When he sat up in bed he cringed in pain from the abuse he had sustained from the gunmen. He held his ribs to stop the agony. He looked in the mirror and didn't recognize the person with two black eyes staring back at him. His face was swollen and covered in dark bruises. After a very long, hot shower he was ready to face his parents.

Carter had told them very little about how he had sustained his injuries before arriving last night. His mom had given him an ice pack before he crawled into bed exhausted. He was dreading telling them, after just returning to their lives, that he would be disappearing again. He walked downstairs and stopped by the study door. He was surprised to see his dad still home from work.

"Morning, Dad. You didn't have to stay home from work on my account."

"I have a good staff. They can manage without me for a few hours so I can visit with my son. How are you feeling?"

"A little stiff, but rested. Thanks for letting me stay here last night. Is Mom around?"

"Yes, she's in the kitchen fixing us some breakfast."

"I need to discuss something with you both."

Carter entered the kitchen and was greeted by a smile from his mom. "I hope you're hungry. I made eggs, grits, and bacon for breakfast this morning."

"It smells awesome. I'm starved."

They sat at the kitchen table and Carter devoured his breakfast while he explained his possible new job with the FBI.

"That is wonderful news, honey! I always knew you were meant for more than just a detective," his Mom said.

His dad remained quiet while he continued. "I know you just met your grandson but we're going to have to disappear for a while. The man I just put behind bars is the one responsible for what happened to my face. He has gone to great lengths to quiet everyone that has testified against him. I'm just praying he won't go after you. The FBI is giving Sophia, Jose, and I a new identity so we'll be safe. We're going to relocate somewhere in Georgia. I have to leave today to meet up with them. Once we are settled in our new home I'll find a way to communicate with you and let you know we are okay."

Carter's dad finally spoke, "Is there anything we can do to help?"

"You've already done so much with flying Jose to Miami and letting us stay in your condo. I have to pick up a new burner phone today and I'll make sure you have the number before I leave. But only call in case of an emergency. In fact, I just thought of a way we can keep in touch. When I get my new identity, I'll call your office. I'll say I'm interested in your financial guidance. You can sign me up as a new client so communicating with me under my new name won't raise any suspicions. That'll also give you an excuse to visit me in Georgia. You'll have to set up a meeting with your new client. What do you think?"

"That should work. You'll be in our database and I'll make sure there are some funds in your account so no one suspects."

"Good. Then you should hear from me in a few weeks under my new name. I love you both, even though I haven't shown it in a while. Unfortunately, I must be leaving. I need to return the rental car, pick up my mustang and bird from Rosa, then turn in my badge before heading north."

Carter's mom had been quiet this whole time. "Son, you know all your father and I have ever wanted is for you to be happy. Sophia seems to bring you that happiness. Make sure she knows that and don't let her out of your life again."

"She and Jose have definitely changed my life. I haven't any intention of letting her go and hope you'll be able to attend our wedding." Carter gave his parents one last, quick hug. He wanted to get away before his mom started to cry.

"Take care son. Don't hesitate to call if you need us," Carter's dad said.

His dad firmly shook Carter's hand before letting him go. Carter looked back before driving away. His unemotional dad had his arm securely wrapped around his mom's shoulders, offering her the comfort and support she needed. Dad had softened over the years. It was much more difficult to leave this time.

***

Rosa pulled up to the rental car place in Carter's mustang. She spotted Carter standing by the curb with his few belongings by his side. She drove up next to him and surrendered the driver's seat. "Looks like you had a rough night. What happened to you?"

"Dragone wasn't happy with his sentence and sent two guys to take it out on me."

From the back seat Rosco chimed in on cue, "Bad guys, bang, bang."

"Yes. Rosco, the bad guys are dead. I hope Rosco wasn't too much trouble."

"No, not at all. I'm going to miss him. I started looking forward to his unusual greeting when I walked in the door. It's going to be quiet with him gone."

"I know what you mean. He kind of grows on you."

"So where are you headed after you resign today?"

"I'm going to have to disappear for a while so I don't get anymore surprises like the one last night." Rosa had been his partner for three years and was like family to him. "I'm sorry to have to leave you like this. I can't repay you for all you've done. Jose is going to be so sorry that he won't see you again."

"I'll miss him, too. Let him know, even though we won't see each other, I'll be thinking of him."

"Watch your back. I wouldn't put it past Dragone to have his men harass people I know to try to find me or Marcus. Also, there may still be some more moles in the department that the FBI haven't yet caught. Be careful with any new men that might come into your life."

Carter pulled into the parking area of the police station and hesitated before opening the door. "You're a very special person. I hope you find a man that can take your abuse after a long day, that'll be there for you." Carter smiled, trying to ease the tension between them.

"They don't make a man that can put up with me," Rosa laughed.

Carter couldn't delay any longer. He grabbed his badge and removed his service revolver from his shoulder holster. He walked to the captain's office and recognized the man behind the desk. He had worked with him on a case a few years back. He was very professional and smart. He had pointed some things out at the crime scene that Carter had missed. Carter knew he would make a good captain. He placed his badge and service revolver on the captain's desk. "I won't be needing these anymore. Find Rosa a good partner that won't let her down."

The captain saw the bruises on Carter's face. No further explanation was needed. "Take care. I wish you the best. If you ever want to come back, there'll be an opening for you."

Carter stopped on his way out to hug Rosa one last time. "Thanks again for always having my back. Stay out of harms way." Carter avoided the stares and walked out without looking back.

Carter stopped at a used car dealership on his way north. He negotiated an even trade for a four door nondescript beige Toyota sedan with low miles. The mustang brought too much attention and was easy to follow. He made good time on the interstate and arrived at the address Alex had given him in Georgia just after eleven. The house was dark so Carter approached cautiously. The front door opened and Alex came out with his gun by his side.

"I didn't recognize the vehicle." He lowered his weapon.

"Sorry, I decided to change cars on my way up. I wanted to be as inconspicuous as possible. Thought this car would help me to blend in and reduce the risk of being followed."

"Good idea. Those guys really did a number on your face. There are some anxious people inside that have been waiting for you to arrive."

Alex opened the door for Carter. He was greeted by a round of hugs and kisses from Sophia and Jose. After assuring everyone that he was fine, he handed Jose a gift. It was a baseball bat, mitt and ball.

Jose was all smiles. He proceeded to tell Carter about his latest adventure, traveling to Georgia.

Carter was thrilled to hear all the details and to see Jose's face light up as he told him about getting to eat donuts for breakfast. He was thrilled to see Jose so energetic. "Glad to hear you're having fun. It's very late, though, and I'm sure way past your bedtime. How about I put you to bed and you can tell me the rest in the morning?" Carter tucked Jose in bed and stayed with him for a little while until he fell asleep. It was still hard to believe he had a son.

Carter found Sophia all by herself in the kitchen baking, something she does when she is upset. He reached for her hands so that she would look at him. "How are you doing?" Carter asked.

"Much better than you obviously," Sophia replied.

"I'm not sure how much Alex shared with you but the two men that did this won't come looking for me again."

"Alex just told me that you had a situation to deal with before leaving Miami.
That you were running a little late. That's all."

"Not to worry. We're all safe now. No one knows where I am except you."

178

Before they could continue with their reunion, Alex approached. "I need to bring you up to speed on our plan."

"Is it okay if Sophia stays?"

"Sure. You'll probably want to tell her anyway. The two men that did this to your face weren't able to share who hired them before they died. But we all know Dragone was behind it. With him behind bars his influence should be diminished. His men will not stay loyal for long. Next, everyone's new identity was issued today. This is yours." Alex handed Carter a file. "Memorize this resume. Your new name is Adam Booker. You grew up in Jefferson City, Missouri where you graduated from the University of Missouri with a masters degree in psychology. You were a teacher before joining the FBI as a profiler."

"A profiler? That's what I'm going to be doing?"

"Yes, does that sound too boring after the last few weeks?"

"No, that's not it at all. I just hope I don't disappoint anyone, since I know very little about psychology."

"You would be surprised how much you've picked up over the years investigating murder. The FBI will teach you everything you need to know. Next, there is a farm northeast of Atlanta. The property has two homes and is roughly one hundred acres in size. Since Marcus has cash we have expedited the closing. He's going to close under his new identity tomorrow."

"Wow! That fast. You guys work miracles. When do I start my training?"

"I'm afraid you don't have much time here. In three days you need to be in Virginia."

Carter looked over at Sophia and squeezed her hand. "It'll only be until I finish my training. Then I'll be back before you know it."

"I understand. I'll keep myself busy settling into our new home, finding a job and a school for Jose to attend."

"Don't rush to find work. Give yourself a chance to enjoy your new life. You've worked hard all your life and deserve a break. With my big FBI salary I can cover your expenses," he laughed.

"We'll see. I'm not good at sitting around doing nothing."

"Believe me, Marcus is going to need your help around the farm. You won't get bored."

Alex excused himself. "Try to get some rest. The next few days are going to be hectic."

Now alone, Carter faced Sophia with her hand still in his. "I've missed you." He leaned over and kissed her passionately.

She responded without hesitation. Realizing their privacy could be interrupted at any time, with a house full of people, she pushed back. "We'll have plenty of time to catch up once we move into our own place. Good night. I'll see you in the morning."

Carter stole one last kiss before retreating to his bedroom. He collapsed on the bed, with his head overflowing with information. It wasn't going to be easy adjusting to being Adam Booker for the rest of his life.

***

The next three days passed too fast for Carter. The closing went without a hitch and Sophia's family started their new lives by getting settled into their homes. Marcus, Maria, their two sons, and Nana moved into a large, white, two story farmhouse with four bedrooms. At the other end of the property Carter helped Sophia and Jose move into a smaller two bedroom, yellow painted wood frame home. It had a large wraparound porch with a swing hanging from the porch ceiling. The view was heavenly, with rolling hills in every direction. Sophia loved the finished basement where the laundry room was located. She planned to set up a table in the basement to make herself a sewing room. The home was a little bigger than their place in Belize. There was plenty of room for Jose to run and play outside without any worries.

Before moving in, Sophia insisted they scrub everything from top to bottom. The smell of bleach filled the air. When everything was finally sparkling clean they went shopping. Carter maxed out his new charge card but had a blast doing so. He had so much fun seeing the excitement in Jose's eyes as they picked out his bedroom furniture. The furniture was scheduled for delivery the next day. They arrived home exhausted, with bags of kitchen items, linens, curtains, and clothes filling every crevasse of Carter's car. Sophia excused herself to start unpacking the kitchen.

Carter looked over at Rosco sitting on top of his cage in the corner of the empty living room. Any time Jose giggled Rosco laughed back, which only made Jose giggle even more. "I have a big favor to ask of you, buddy. Do you think you could take care of Rosco for me while I'm gone?"

"Really, I can have him while you're away?" Jose asked.

"You have to talk to him every day and not let him get bored. I'm sure you could teach him a few new words for me."

Rosco repeated what Carter said, "Rosco bored."

They both laughed. While Jose talked to Rosco, Carter disappeared into the kitchen to find Sophia. They had had very little time alone since he arrived. Sophia was busy cleaning all the new dishes she bought and stocking the kitchen cabinets.

"I missed you," Carter said as he placed his arms around her waist from behind.

Sophia smiled and turned around to face him. She kissed him on the lips.

"I promised you a date. How would you like to go out tomorrow night before I leave? Maria and Marcus can watch Jose for a few hours."

"That sounds nice."

"Great! Wear your nicest dress. I'm going to take you somewhere special."

"I've only purchased a few clothes. You'll have to be satisfied with a skirt and blouse."

"When I get back from training we'll go on another shopping spree just for you. I know how much you've sacrificed for Jose. I want to make it up to you."

"Nonsense. Everything I do for Jose is out of love and isn't a sacrifice."

"I know. I just meant you deserve something nice and I want to buy it for you."

Sophia wasn't used to having someone buy her things. "I would like that."

"Good, now that that is settled, it's late and unpacking can wait until tomorrow. Let's join Jose by the fireplace." Carter dragged Sophia away from the cluttered kitchen.

That night they camped out on a rug covered floor in front of the fireplace. Even though it was a warm night, Carter lit a fire so they could roast marshmallows. They laughed more than they had laughed in a long time. After their busy day, Jose was no longer able to keep his eyes open. He fell asleep in front of the warm fire. Sophia covered him with his new comforter decorated with airplanes.

Carter and Sophia snuggled together in their makeshift bed on the floor. They fell asleep in each other's arms.

***

The next day Carter did an internet search for restaurants in the area and found a five star steak house about thirty minutes away. The furniture arrived just before lunch. He spent time the rest of the afternoon assembling beds and dressers with Jose's help. Then Jose said something that made his day.

"Daddy, could I move Rosco in here with me while you're gone?"

Carter smiled to himself. Jose had accepted him as his father. "Yes, of course. Rosco would love the company. Rosco is an early riser, though. He may wake you up when the sun comes up. He's very chatty first thing in the morning." Carter looked at his watch and realized it was almost time for his date with Sophia. "Hey buddy, I'm going to take you to Maria and Marcus' house to play with your cousins. You will eat supper with them tonight. I've planned something special for your mother. Is that okay?"

182

Jose, with a big smile on his face, asked, "Are you going to ask her to marry you?"

"What if I said yes, would that be all right with you?"

"Of course it would be. You're part of our family now."

It was difficult sometimes to imagine that Jose was only eleven years old. He acted so mature and logical for a boy his age. But most boys his age haven't gone through what he has, Carter thought. "Gather up anything you would like to take with you. We better get going."

Sophia walked into the room wearing her new knee length, flowery skirt with a white blouse and sandals. She weaved her long brunette hair into a French braid, leaving just a few curly strands framing her face. "Wow! Doesn't your mom look nice?"

"You sure do, Mama."

"Well, thank you. Are you ready to go to Aunt Maria and Uncle Marcus'?"

"Yes. Let me just say goodbye to Rosco first. Goodbye Rosco. Don't be scared. I'll be back soon."

"Goodbye," Rosco repeated.

They arrived at the restaurant a little after seven. There were linen tablecloths and napkins along with a centerpiece of fresh wildflowers on each table. Carter ordered a bottle of merlot and an appetizer to start their evening. They talked the night away, catching up on the last eleven years.

Sophia had so many stories of how rambunctious Jose was growing up. "From the time he started to walk till now he has always been curious about everything. I couldn't take my eyes off of him for a second or he would get into trouble. At school the teachers would get on to him for not paying attention and daydreaming. I just don't think school challenged him enough."

"Hopefully he will attend a school here that will give him lessons difficult enough to occupy his mind. He starts school next week, which is good. I'm sure he'll make all kinds of new friends. Has he been having any more nightmares?"

"No, this move has been really good for him. I've been keeping him so busy he hasn't had time to dwell on what he has been through."

"Good." Carter became very serious. "I want you to know that I'm not leaving you again. I have to go through a very aggressive eight week training session, and I may not be able to call you every night. Believe me, I'll be thinking of you though. I'll be back before you have time to finish decorating the house."

"I know," Sophia said with a sad look across her face.

Carter reached across the table for Sophia's hand. "I can't make up for my past mistakes but I hope you'll let me try." Carter released Sophia's hand just long enough to pull a small box from the pocket of his suit.

"What are you doing?" Sophia asked.

"I know you aren't ready to marry me yet, but I wanted to give you this ring." Carter gave the box to Sophia.

She opened the lid and gasped at the beautiful ring. "This is too much."

"This was my grandmother's wedding ring. I want you to have it as a promise that I'm going to be in your life as long as you'll have me. I don't want to push you into something you aren't ready for, but when you are ready, I'll be waiting to marry you." Carter slid the ring onto her finger. It was a simple silver band with a beautiful two carat diamond setting.

Sophia held up her hand, admiring how it looked on her finger. "Thank you for giving me time to adjust to the idea of marriage. I've never stopped loving you. I've enjoyed getting to know you again."

Carter leaned over the table and kissed Sophia passionately. He held up his wine glass and made a toast. "To the most beautiful, courageous, woman I know. Leaving you was the worst mistake of my life. To growing old together and making up for lost time. Cheers!"

***

Carter completed his rigorous training and was assigned to the FBI office in Atlanta as planned. After training he moved in with Sophia and Jose and commuted back and forth to Atlanta each day. It wasn't long before Sophia agreed to marry him. With Carter's new identity in place, he contacted his father. He signed up as a new client as planned. This enabled Carter to invite his parents to the wedding. They flew into Atlanta and Carter met them outside the baggage terminal. The reunion was full of hugs and kisses from his mother, who was full of questions about the wedding. She understood that they had to keep it intimate and private. The ceremony was held at a small, local Catholic church. Carter's parents surprised them with a generous wedding gift, a prepaid honeymoon suite with spa treatment included, along with two gift certificates to fancy restaurants in downtown Atlanta. After the wedding, Carter's parents wanted to get to know their grandson better. They asked to stay with him while Carter and Sophia were on their honeymoon.

Carter's dad took Jose flying in a small private plane, to Jose's delight. Jose was immediately hooked and wanted to get his pilot license as soon as he turned sixteen.

Jose excelled in his new school and loved science. There was no limit to what he could become.

Not long after returning from their honeymoon, Sophia found out that she was pregnant. Jose was going to have the brother he aways wanted.

The farm provided a good source of income for Maria and Marcus. They grew corn on part of the land and raised cows on the other half. Their two sons loved living on the farm and working around the many animals. Their sons were allowed to each pick a puppy from the local humane society. They both chose puppies with big clumsy feet, floppy ears, and a tail that never stopped wagging. The boys were immediately inseparable from their beloved dogs. Also, a mysterious tiger striped cat appeared one

185

day and joined the household. The cat left evidence of her worth each morning by strategically placing a dead rat by the back door.

Their new identities kept them safe. There had been no more threats. They didn't have to live their lives in fear ever again.

Jose still sneaked out his bedroom window most nights to lay in the cool grass and watch the blinking lights coming from the jets flying high above his head. He heard the distant roar of their engines as they passed. No longer did he imagine being on one of those jets, taking him to a far away exciting place. His dream had already come true.

About The Author

Diane E. Izzard lives in Welaka, Florida near the St. Johns River. The laid back Florida life style provides her the inspiration she needs to write. She has a bachelor degree in Industrial Engineering and master degree in Management. She worked at Kennedy Space Center until 2013 when she started her writing career. She loves dogs, hiking, biking, skiing, and curling up with a good book. Her latest dog, an Alaskan Malamute, provides the personality for the dogs in some of her stories. Visit her on Facebook at www.facebook.com/Dianee.Izzard.

www.ingramcontent.com/pod-product-compliance
Lightning Source LLC
Chambersburg PA
CBHW071911220626
47052CB00002B/301